KB067768

사랑하라, 희망 없이

아시아에서는 《바이링궐 에디션 한국 대표 소설》을 기획하여 한국의 우수한 문학을 주제별로 엄선해 국내외 독자들에게 소개합니다. 이 기획은 국내외 우수한 번역가들이 참여하여 원작의 품격을 최대한 살렸습니다. 문학을 통해 아시아의 정체성과 가치를 살피는 데 주력해 온 아시아는 한국인의 삶을 넓고 깊게 이해하는 데 이 기획이 기여하기를 기대합니다.

Asia Publishers presents some of the very best modern Korean literature to readers worldwide through its new Korean literature series ⟨Bilingual Edition Modern Korean Literature⟩. We are proud and happy to offer it in the most authoritative translation by renowned translators of Korean literature. We hope that this series helps to build solid bridges between citizens of the world and Koreans through a rich in-depth understanding of Korea.

바이링궐 에디션 한국 대표 소설 062

Bi-lingual Edition Modern Korean Literature 062

Love, Hopelessly

윤영수
사랑하라, 희망 없이

Yun Young-su

ASIA
PUBLISHERS

Contents

사랑하라, 희망 없이

Love, Hopelessly

1

「도망가요! 그런데, 꼬리가 잘리면 두 마리가 되는 거예요?」

꼬리? 지렁이 꼬리? 도대체 나는 무슨 뚱딴지같은 질문을 해대었는지.

잠에서 깨어나 처음 눈에 띈 것은, 여느 때와 다름없이 아스타일이 축축 처진 우리 방의 천장이다. 저 정도의 직사각형 아스타일이라면 처음부터 나사를 여섯 개박았어야 했다. 자잘한 나사를 네 귀퉁이에만 겨우 박

1

"Let's run away! But, by the way, if you cut it where the tail is, will it become two pieces?"

The tail? Earthworm tail? What was I talking about?

When I open my eyes, the first thing I see is, of course, the ceiling and its drooping asphalt tiles. Given their rectangular shape, it looks like each tile needs at least six screws to remain fastened tightly into the ceiling. But, because only four screws have been used to fasten each tile's four corners, every single tile is drooping at the center as if they were

아놓았으니 배들이 불룩하게 처진다. 이제는 할 수 없다. 가운데에 못을 친다 해도 헛일이다. 공간이 너무 떠서 못이 붙어 있을 수가 없다.

작년 가을, 서울에 처음 올라와 이 방에서 자던 첫날 밤, 나는 저 천장 때문에 너무 놀랐었다. 불을 끄고 누웠는데 천장이 울툭불툭한 것이, 박쥐떼가 잔뜩 들러붙어 있는 줄 알았다—나중에 차분히 생각해보니 그것은 텔레비전 영화의 한 장면이었다. 장소도, 방이 아니라 산 꼭대기의 외진 동굴이었고—나도 모르게 벌떡 일어나 불을 켰다. 천장에는 아무것도 없었다. 창문을 통해 비치는 부유스름한 가로등 불빛에 배가 처진 아스타일들의 그림자가 뒤얽혀 그렇게 괴이쩍게 보였던 것이다. 겨우 마음을 가라앉히고 형광등 스위치를 다시 내리기는 했지만 편안히 잠들 수는 없었다. 지렁이. 자세히 살펴본 천장의 아스타일에는 한 장에도 수십 마리의 지렁이, 그것도 토막토막 끊어진 갯지렁이가 구불구불 새겨져 있었다. 처진 아스타일마다 갯지렁이가 수북수북 쌓여, 잠이 들기만 하면 내 몸 위에 쏟아져 내려, 겨드랑이고 배고 할 것 없이 그것들이 스멀대는 환상에 뜬눈으

all sporting little pot bellies. At this point, there's clearly no fixing them. Even if you were to nail each tile down in in the middle, the nails wouldn't stay in place because of the drooping space between the ceiling and each tile.

On the first night I slept here on my first trip to Seoul last fall, I was surprised at what I thought I saw on the ceiling. When I lay down in the dark, the drooping ceiling looked as if there were bats hanging from all over it (Later, when I calmed down and thought about it, I realized that I was thinking of a scene in a movie I'd seen on TV. The scene wasn't set in a room, but a remote cave on a mountaintop). I got up abruptly and turned on the light. There was nothing on the ceiling. A faint light from the street lamps must have come in through the window and turned the shadows of the drooping asphalt tiles into those grotesque shapes. Although I managed to calm down and turn off the florescent light, I wasn't able to fall back asleep very easily. Earthworms. When I looked at the asphalt tiles carefully, I could see the hordes of earthworms—or, to be more precise, the army of tiny lugworm with their many contorting joints carved across the tiles. For a moment, I felt like these deceptively lifelike lugworms, accumu-

11

로 꼬박 밤을 지새우고 말았다. 그러고 보면 사람은 확실히 환경에 적응하는 동물이다. 보름도 채 되지 않아 나는 축축 처진 천장에 익숙해졌다. 늘어진 아스타일들의 곡선이 어찌 보면 고향 마을 앞바다에 쉴 새 없이 밀려오는 물결 같아서 반갑기까지 하다. 그렇지만 지렁이에까지 익숙해진 건 아니다. 길쯤하고 끈끈하고 물컹거리는 지렁이는 언제나 지렁이일 뿐이다. 희고 반듯한 아스타일에 하필이면 지렁이무늬를 찍어 파는 사람들의 심사를 나는 아직도 이해할 수가 없다.

세상에! 꿈속에서 둥둥대던 북소리가 그대로 들린다. 이럴 수가.

비…… 비가 온다. 꿈속에서 나던 북소리는 이제 생각해보니 빗소리다.

건물 뒤쪽에 있는 털보 아저씨네 한옥 지붕 위로, 우리 건물 옥상의 빗물이 모여 떨어지는 소리다. 옥상 난간을 에두른 빗물받이에 구멍이 나서 제법 굵은 물줄기가 삼층 높이에서 포물선을 그리며 떨어지는 것이다. 물줄기가 떨어지는 한옥 지붕 위에는 녹이 잔뜩 슨 함석판 하나가 얹혀 있다. 비가 올 때마다 그 함석판이 뚱

lated across the expanse of those drooping asphalt tiles, would rain down writhing all over my body at any second, burrowing under my armpits and belly, creeping in the moment I fell back asleep. I stayed up all night.

But, people are adaptable. I got used to that droopy ceiling in less than two weeks. Now I'm even glad. The curvy lines of the drooping asphalt tiles now remind me of the ocean waves of my home village. Still, I'm not getting used to the idea of the lugworms. Long, sticky, viscous lugworms. They're lugworms no matter what. I still can't understand why people would choose to carve that lugworm pattern into those square, white asphalt tiles.

My God! I can still hear the drumbeat I'd heard in my dream. What the hell?

Rain. It's raining. I realize that the drumbeat in my dream was, in fact, the sound of this rain.

It was the sound of rain gathering on the rooftop of the building I lived in and dripping non-stop on the tiled roof of the hairy uncle's traditional-style house behind our building. A thick stream of rainwater must have been falling through a hole in the gutter surrounding the edges of the rooftop. There's

땅뚱땅 요동을 친다. 시끄럽긴 하지만 지붕 위에 함석판을 올려놓은 것은 잘한 짓이다. 그나마 함석판을 얹지 않았더라면 과자처럼 바삭바삭한 헌 기와 지붕이 벌써 예전에 거덜이 나버렸을 게 분명하다.

건물 주인은 아무것도 모른다. 자기 식구들이 여기서 살지 않으니 비가 올 때마다 얼마나 뒤숭숭한지, 뒤채 지붕이 얼마나 위태로운지 도통 관심이 없다. 빗소리도 소리지만, 다 쓰러져가는 한옥 역시 자기 소유인데 그집 식구들이 다치기라도 하면 어쩌려는지 알 수 없다. 우리 이층 방에서 내려다보면, 기와 틈을 비집고 자란 쑥부쟁이 키가 일 미터는 된다. 시골의 허물어져가는 폐가라면 몰라도 사람 사는 집치고 이렇게 몰골 흉한 기와집도 드물 것이다. 건물 주인은 이삼 층 건물을 지으면서 준공이 되는 대로 한옥을 철거할 생각이었다는데, 막상 건물을 다 짓고 보니 또 아까운 생각이 들어서 그냥 두었다고 한다. 말이야 〈전셋돈도 수월치 않은 털보 아저씨네 사정 보아주느라고〉였다지만, 그래서 털보 아저씨네가 보수 운운할 때마다 고칠 것도 없이 그만 허물어버리겠다고 협박 아닌 협박을 하는 모양이지만,

a heavily rusted sheet of zinc on that rooftop. Whenever it rains, that sheet of zinc begins to rock and groan. Although it's noisy, it was a good thing that they covered the roof with that sheet of zinc. But for that sheet, that fragile old tile roof, as brittle as a roof of crackers, would have already given in long ago.

Our landlord knows nothing about this. Since it isn't his family living here, he doesn't care a bit about how unsettling it is to us whenever it rains, or how precarious the roof of the house behind our building is. He also owns that house behind our building. I wonder why he's not worried about the possibility of the family living in that house getting hurt, although the noise wouldn't bother him. When I look down at the house from our room on the second floor, I can see starworts overgrown all over the tiled roof, some as high as a meter tall. Except for some abandoned, crumbling houses in the countryside, there won't be too many inhabited houses as decrepit as this one. People said that the landlord originally planned to demolish that tradi-tional-style home as soon as he finished building this three-story building, but he changed his mind after the building was completed. He must not

15

주인이 쉽사리 한옥을 허물지는 않을 것이라고 주방 아줌마는 단언한다.

한옥에서 들어오는 월세가 얼만데? 택도 없지.

아줌마는 자기 입장이라도 어림없다는 듯 찌부러진 눈을 부릅뜬다.

주인 욕할 거 뭐 있어. 그럼, 한 군데 샌다고 옥상 전체 빗물받이를 온통 갈아? 윤희, 네년이 뭣 땜에 흥분하니? 지붕이야 거덜이 나건 말건 네가 거기서 자지도 않으면서.

마담 언니는 한가하게 손톱을 다듬으며 종알거린다. 건물에 두른 플라스틱 빗물받이가 십여 년 전의 구형이라, 똑같은 마디를 구할 수가 없다는 것이다.

건물 일층 점포에서 표구집을 하는 털보 아저씨네는 풍을 맞은 할머니까지 여섯 식구다. 점포 안쪽 구석에 궤짝처럼 쌓아올린 연탄 구들에서 털보 아저씨 내외와 여섯 살짜리 막내가 자고, 건물 뒷문에 달아 붙은 이 낡은 한옥에서는 아이들 둘과 할머니가 잔다. 비가 올 때마다 뚱땅대는 소리를 참고 사는 걸 보면 그 집 식구들 성질도 어지간하다.

have wanted to part with what little rent he got from it. Although, he claimed that he "wanted to help the hairy uncle's family who were too poor to afford a higher rent for some other housing."

Auntie, who works our kitchen, claims the landlord would only very reluctantly demolish that traditional-style building, despite his threats that he would rather demolish it if the hairy uncle asked for repairs.

"You know how much income the rent from that house means? He can't just give that up!" Auntie glares with her crooked eye, as if to say *she* wouldn't do it, either. Sister, the coffee shop owner, prattles on about the old house, too, leisurely polishing her nails while doing so.

"Why blame the landlord? Why replace the entire gutter when there's just a single hole? Yun-hi, why are you so worried? Whether the roof gives in or not, *you* aren't sleeping in that house."

According to her, there were no replacement parts available for that ten-year-old old-fashioned plastic gutter of this building.

The hairy uncle owns a frame shop on the fist floor of our building. His is a family of six, including a granny who'd just suffered a stroke. The hairy

군악대가 지나가던 꿈속의 거리는 바로 우리 골목 바깥, 마로니에 공원 앞길이다. 맨 끝줄, 작은 북을 멘 군인 하나가 다른 대원들하고 자꾸 발이 어긋난다. 거리의 구경꾼들이 그를 보고 킥킥거린다. 얼굴이 벌개진 그는 발걸음을 고쳐보려고도 하지만 그의 걸음걸이는 다른 이와 영 맞지 않는다. 그 와중에도 북소리는 여전하다. 아니다. 그가 북을 두드리는 것이 아니다. 자세히 보면 그의 손이 아니라 북채 짓이다. 자동으로 움직이는 북채에 그의 흰 손이 들러붙어 있다.

주위의 구경꾼들이 제각기 딴청을 부리면서 한 발짝씩 그에게 다가선다. 자기들끼리 무슨 음모라도 꾸민 눈치다. 그가 드디어 군중들에게 갇힌다. 그는 당황하여 자신의 발을 내려다본다. 흰 모자 밑으로 보이는 그의 관자놀이에 불끈불끈 솟는 힘줄이 이제는 애원에 가깝다. 그의 군악대는 어느새 길 저 끝으로 사라져간다. 그는 주위 사람들의 몸에 파묻혀 일행을 쳐다볼 수도 없다.

꿈속에서 북을 치던 군인은 이제 생각해보니 분명히 박 선생님이었다. 흰 모자, 흰 제복에 반짝이는 금단추,

uncle, his wife, and their five-year-old son sleep in a tiny room equipped with Korean hypocaust system in the back corner of his store. The room looks more like a few stacked crates than a real room. Their two other children and their granny sleep in the old house. Judging by the way they live in that house, barely making a peep even when it rattles and groans in the rain, they must be a pretty patient family.

The street where the marching band was passing by in my dream is the main street in front of Marronnier Park outside of our alley. In the last row of the marching band, a soldier beating a small drum kept missing his steps. The spectators giggled. His face flushed, the soldier tried to correct his steps, but he was too clumsy to fit in. He doesn't skip the drumbeat, though. Actually, it wasn't him who was beating his drum. Upon closer examination, it turned out that it was just his drumsticks. The drumsticks were moving up and down automatically, and the drummer's pale hands were attached to them. The spectators slowly approached him, one step at a time, feigning disinterest. It seemed that they had all conspired to make some mischief. At last, the soldier was completely surrounded by

양어깨에 금빛 술을 늘어뜨린 군악대의 제복이 그의 하
얗고 긴 손가락에 정말 제격이었다. 뿐만 아니다. 주위
에 둘러선 구경꾼 중에는 털보 아저씨, 머리가 반쯤 벗
겨진 안경집 아저씨, 언니, 맞다. 웬일로 겨울 밍크코트
를 두른 새빨간 입술의 언니도 섞여 있었다. 갑자기 억
울하다. 내가 잘 아는 사람들이 여럿 등장하는 꿈에서
깨게 되면, 꿈이었다는 생각이 들지 않고 나만 내쫓고
자기들끼리 무슨 짓을 계속하는 것 같아 괜히 부아가
난다.

도망가요!

그를 깔아뭉개듯 점점 좁혀드는 사람들 틈새에 대고
나는 입나팔을 만들어 크게 소리를 쳤다. 거기까지는
좋았는데 꼬리가 잘리다니, 박 선생님에게 무슨 꼬리?
꿈이니 망정이지 내가 외치는 소리를 박 선생님이 실제
로 들었더라면 큰일 날 뻔했다.

드러누운 채로 팔과 다리를 쭉 편다. 아침에 기지개를
한껏 펴면 키가 커진다고 한다. 오 센티만 더 크면 좋겠
다. 그러면 백육십이 센티. 키 큰 여자가 겉늙는다고 백
육십오 센티인 언니는 투덜거리지만, 언니 얼굴에 잔주

the crowd. Completely taken aback, he looked down at his feet. The veins on his temples under his white hat bulged out, looking almost like they're pulsing in protest to the leering crowd. The man's band was already far away. Buried within the crowd, he couldn't even follow them with his eyes.

Come to think of it, the soldier beating the drum in my dream was clearly Mr. Park. The white hat, the shiny golden buttons attached to the white uniform, and the shoulder pieces with their dangling golden tassels—his uniform went so well with his pale tapering fingers. Besides him, there was the hairy uncle, the bald eyeglass store guy, and Sister —that's right, Sister with her red-hot lips and in a mink coat for some reason—among the spectators. Suddenly, I feel upset. Whenever I wake up from a dream where many of my acquaintances appear, I feel unreasonably upset. It doesn't feel like a dream. Instead, I feel like it just keeps going on even after they kick me out.

"Let's run away!" I made my hands into a megaphone and hollered through them. I tried shouting through a crack in the crowd that was inching in on him as if to smother him. That's all good and fine, but what did I mean by "Cut it where the tail is?"

름이 많이 잡히는 것은 원래 언니의 체질인 것 같다. 이제 서른한 살, 하루 종일 얼굴만 매만지는 정성에 비하면, 언니 얼굴은 말대로 〈구제불능〉이다. 화장을 많이 한 피부라 그럴까, 웃기만 하면 뚜렷이 패이는 눈가의 부챗살들은 내가 보기에도 안쓰러운 감이 있다.

한숨이 나온다. 박 선생님 머릿속에는 언니밖에 없다. 그는 내 마음을 몰라도 너무 모른다. 바보 같은 박 선생님. 하기야 나는 내 마음도 잘 모른다. 내가 생각해보아도 나는 변덕이 너무 심하다. 보통 때에는 사람들에게 멀쩡히 잘 대해주다가도 어느 한순간에는 이유도 없이 속이 부글부글 끓어올라 눈 한번 곱게 떠지지 않는다. 그래도 삼층 신문보급소의 현수는 싱글벙글이다. 톡톡 뱉는 내 말버릇이 매력이라나? 어울리지도 않게 능글거리기는. 아무리 젠 체해도 현수는 불합격이다. 토끼띠, 스무 살. 풋내가 풀풀 난다. 남자라면 박 선생님 정도는 되어야 믿음직하다. 올해로 서른둘, 토끼라도 늙은 토끼다. 나하고는 열네 살 차이. 나이가 무슨 상관이람? 어떤 여류화가는 자기보다 마흔 살이나 많은 남자하고 결혼해서도 잘만 산다고 한다.

What tail was I talking about for Mr. Park? I'm glad it was a dream, because it would have been a disaster, if Mr. Park really heard what I was shouting at him.

Still lying down, I stretch out my arms and legs. They say if you stretch in the morning, you get taller. I hope I can get just five centimeters taller. Then I'll be 160 cm. Sister grumbles, claiming that a tall woman gets older faster than anyone else. But, in my opinion, she's just wrinkled by nature. She's only thirty now. Her face must be literally irredeemable when you consider all the care she's put into it. Maybe, it's because she put too much make-up on? The crow's feet that appear around her eyes whenever she smiles make me feel sorry for her.

I sigh without intending to. All Mr. Park thinks about is Sister. He doesn't know my feelings at all. Not at all. How stupid of him! But the fact of the matter is that I don't know my feelings that well, either. I'm too fickle. Sometimes I get mad for no reason at people I'm usually friendly with. In those times, I can't look them straight in the eye. Nevertheless, Hyeon-su at the newspaper delivery office on the third floor is always all smiles with me. He

껄적대는 현수에 비하자면 도리어 박 선생님이 순진하기 짝이 없다. 박 선생님이 언니에게 온통 넋이 팔려 있는 것도 따지고 보면 그가 터무니없이 순진하기 때문이다. 언니의 그 천박한 웃음, 아무에게나 요사를 떨어대는 짓거리라니. 교양이나 인품을 보아도 언니가 박 선생님의 배필은 아니다. 호칭문제만 해도 그렇다. 처음에 내가 언니를 아줌마라고 부르니까 그렇게 언짢아했다. 어디를 봐서 자기가 아줌마 소리 듣게 됐냐는 것이다. 우리 엄마하고 육촌간이면 아무리 나이가 어려도 내게는 아줌마가 아니고 뭐냔 말이다. 하여간 나는 아줌마를 언니라고 부른다. 뭐, 편한 점도 있다. 아줌마라고 하면 아무래도 좀 행동이 어려울 텐데, 언니라고 하니까 대하기가 만만한 게 사실이다.

두고 보시라. 박 선생님은 얼마 안 가서 내 애인이 된다. 말이야 바른 말이지, 언니야 어쨌거나 산전수전 다 겪은 술집여자다. 점점 진하고 야해지는 얼굴 화장이라니, 그런다고 이미 잡힌 주름살이 어디 가나? 박 선생님이 받아주니까 그 얼굴에 별 강짜를 다 부린다. 언니야 사실 나하고는 비교도 안 된다. 열여덟. 누가 봐도 나는

claims that my sharp tongue is so attractive! It really doesn't become him to try to be so sly. No matter how much he puffs himself up, Hyeon-su can't pass my test. Born in the year of rabbit. Twenty years old. Smelling so much like fresh young greens.

A man should be like Mr. Park. Only someone like him is dependable. He's thirty-two. He was also born in the year of rabbit, but he's older than Hyeon-su. So, he's fourteen years older than me. What's the big deal about our age difference anyways? I heard that a painter who married a man forty years her senior was living just fine with him.

In comparison to Hyeon-su, who's always trying to get on my good side or even accidentally cop a feel, Mr. Park is rather innocent. The only reason why he's so enchanted by Sister is that he's so naïve. Her superficial laughs, and her flirts. Gosh! In education or in character, she can't hold a candle to him. You only have to think about the way she reacted when I called her by a different title. When I first called her Auntie, she was so upset. According to her, how could she be an Auntie with the way she looked? But if she's my mom's cousin, she's my aunt, right? Anyway, I have to call her Sister,

이슬을 갓 머금은 장미 꽃봉오리다! 시집가면 하루도 못 살고 내쫓길 거라고? 보내기만 해보시지, 박 선생님 뒷바라지만큼은 거뜬히 해낸다.

비. 비가 온다.

가만히 귀 기울이면, 헌 함석판에 떨어지는 빗물의 간격이 규칙적인 것은 아니다. 소리가 잦아지는 듯싶다가 한순간에 우당퉁탕 시끄럽다. 비. 엊그제 유월에 접어들었으니 장마가 시작인지도 모른다. 비…… 비? 비!

이런, 정신도 참. 우산 생각을 왜 못했을까! 벌떡 몸을 일으켜 시계를 본다. 머리맡의 탁상시계는 아홉 시 사십 분을 막 지나고 있다. 그나마 다행이다. 아직 한 시간 정도는 여유가 있다. 재빨리 이불을 개기 시작한다. 그러고 보니 표구집의 헌 함석판이 고마울 때도 있다. 그렇게 뚱땅거리지 않았더라면 나는 비 오는 것도 모르고 잠만 잘 뻔했다.

이불을 번쩍 들어 윗목의 철제 궤짝에 올려놓는데, 무슨 끈이 팽팽하게 발목에 감긴다. 내 정신 좀 봐, 털실뭉치다. 다행히도 뜨개질거리는 망가지지 않았다. 나는 얼른 입고 있던 잠옷의 가슴 섶 단추를 끄르고 대바늘

not Auntie. It's more convenient that way. If I called her Auntie, then I would have to be more polite towards her. But, since I call her Sister, I can behave more casually towards her.

Well, wait and see! Mr. Park will be my lover soon. Truth be told, Sister is a veteran bar maid no matter what. Just look at her make-up becoming thicker and sexier by the day! That make-up can't hide her wrinkles. With that face of hers, she dares to get unreasonably jealous but only because Mr. Park is so loving towards her. But, actually, you can't compare her with me. I'm eighteen years old. Whoever looks at me can tell that I'm a fresh blooming rose! You say that as a married woman I'd get kicked out before even a day passed? Please, just let me get married! I know I can take care of Mr. Park!

Rain. It's raining.

When you pay attention, you know that the rain doesn't fall on the sheet of zinc in regular intervals. Sometimes, it seems to get slower and quieter, but then the next moment, it hammers down loud. Rain. Now that we're a few days into June, this might be the beginning of our rainy season. Rain... Rain? Rain!

이 덜렁거리는 스웨터자락을 맨젖가슴에 댄다.

「내 젖을 만져요, 자.」

나는 눈을 감으며 나지막하게 중얼거린다. 박 선생님의 하얗고 긴 손이 내 가슴을 부드럽게 어루만진다. 스웨터를 다 짜서 선물하면 박 선생님은 어떤 표정을 지을까. 난생 처음으로 짜기 시작한 스웨터는 한 달 동안 겨우 두 뼘이 넘었다. 젖가슴에 대었던 스웨터자락을 이번에는 얼굴에 댄다. 나도 모르게 한숨이 나온다. 한숨을 자꾸 쉬면 팔자가 세어진다는데.

털실뭉치에서 나는 냄새가 처음에는 참 향긋했었다. 메마른 먼짓내 같으면서도 한편으로는 알싸한 것이, 고향 뒷산 갈대밭에서 나던 풋풋한 수풀 냄새 같았다. 뒷산 갈대밭이라야 특별히 그럴 듯한 곳도 아니었다. 군데군데 고여 있는 물웅덩이, 봄에는 들꽃이 여기저기 피고 가을이면 갈대가 휘날리는, 황량하고 가풀진 언덕이었을 뿐이다. 고향 언덕이 보고 싶거나, 다시 돌아가고픈 것은 아니다. 단지 냄새가 그렇다는 것이다. 나야 어차피 서울에서 살아가야 할 사람이다.

니는 물질 배우지 마래이, 어차피 집 떠날 년 아이가.

Goodness! Why haven't I thought of that umbrella? I jump up and look at the clock. The table clock next to the mattress points to nine forty. I'm not that unlucky. I have about an hour now. I quickly begin to fold my mattress and comforter. Come to think of it, I feel grateful for the old sheet of zinc on top of the framer's roof. If it weren't making all that noise, I probably would have kept on sleeping, not knowing that it was raining at all.

I pick up the folded mattress and comforter and put them down over the steel trunk near the window. At that moment, something that feels like a rope tugs at my ankle. Dear me! It was my ball of yarn. Luckily, I hadn't messed up my knitting project. I quickly unbutton my pajama top and bring the sweater panel I have been knitting onto my naked breasts, knitting needles and all.

"Please, touch me, here!" I close my eyes. Mr. Park's pale tapering fingers touching my breasts softly. When I finish knitting this and give the sweater to Mr. Park, what will his expression be? This being my first knitting project ever, the panel is only about two spans long yet. I move the sweater from my breasts to my face. I sigh. They say that if you sigh too often, you'll run out of luck.

대청 기둥에 걸린 물옷을 입을 때마다 엄마는 성주신 염불 외우듯 같은 말을 되풀이했다.

대처 남자 만나 시집 가그라이. 여 있다 또 남편 물에서 잃고 물길 히젓고 다닐라꼬. 호랭이 굴에 드가도 정신만 차리마 된다캤다. 다방이마 어떻고 술집이마 어떠노.

스웨터에서는 이제 더 이상 풋풋한 수풀 냄새가 나지 않는다. 자꾸 얼굴을 파묻다 보니 로션 냄새가 스웨터 자락에 밴 모양이다. 아쉽긴 하지만 하는 수 없다. 털실 뭉치와 뜨개질거리를 플라스틱 바구니에 담는다. 등판이 끝나면 앞판을 짜고 소매 두 쪽을 짜고…… 부지런히만 뜨면 가을이 가기 전에 끝낼 수 있다고 아줌마가 말했다.

박 선생한테? 그 늙은 글쟁이? 이이런, 젖살도 안 빠진 년이.

주방 아줌마는 가당치도 않다는 듯 배꼽을 잡는다. 〈젖살도 안 빠진 년〉이라니. 우리 엄마가 나를 낳은 나이가 열아홉이다. 뜨개질이나 제대로 가르쳐줄 일이지, 사람들은 별 참견도 다한다.

소리를 죽여가며 살그머니 방문을 연다. 주방 개수대

The yarn smell was really sweet in the beginning. Dry like dust, but pungent as well. It reminded me of a fresh grove I used to smell in the reed field in the back of my home village. That reed field wasn't anything too magnificent. It was a small hill with small puddles here and there. Wild flowers bloomed in the spring and reeds fluttered in the fall. I don't particularly miss that hill in my home village. Nor do I want to go back there. It's just the smell. I have to make my way in Seoul no matter what.

"You shouldn't learn to dive. You're going to leave home anyway, right?" Mom would repeat this over and over as if she was chanting a Buddhist prayer. She'd say this when she'd take down her wet suit from the column in the hall to put it on.

"Meet a city guy and marry him. If you stay here, you'll lose your husband to the sea and end up diving in the sea forever. They say that you can even walk into a lion's den and survive if you just stay calm. I don't care if you start working at a coffee shop or a bar," Mom said.

I can no longer smell the fresh grove from the sweater now, though. Maybe because I buried my face in it too often, the smell of my lotion must

의 수도를 틀고 한창 김칫거리를 씻어대는 아줌마의 뒷모습이 보인다. 슬리퍼를 꿰어 신고는 살금살금 벽을 굽이 돌아 홀 한쪽 구석의 화장실로 향한다. 세면대의 수도를 소리 안 나게 틀고 고양이 세수를 마친다. 다시 방으로 스며들어 문을 조용히 닫는다. 성공. 이만하면 나도 서울 사람이 다 되었다.

니맨쿠로 물러터진 아아는 서울 물 좀 묵으야 한다카이. 우예 좀 똘망똘망해질란강.

엄마가 나를 굳이 서울에 보낸 것도 이런 데 이유가 있었을 것이다. 내가 맡은 차심부름이나 확실히 하면 되었지 주방일까지 도울 의무는 없는 것이다.

주방 아줌마의 자개 경대 앞에 앉는다. 모서리가 닳아 빨간 옻칠이 군데군데 벗겨진 아줌마의 경대 앞에 앉을 때마다 나는 주방 아줌마의 손톱을 보는 듯하다. 아줌마 손톱의 매니큐어는 온전할 날이 없다. 하기는 온종일 물에 손을 담그고 사니 그럴 수밖에 없을 것이다. 그런 아줌마가 코는 좋아서, 언니가 매니큐어를 바르는 것을 귀신같이 알고 쫓아와 자신의 손가락을 내민다. 매니큐어 색깔이 틀리다고 말려도 아줌마는 막무가내다.

have gotten rubbed into it. I feel sorry about that, but there's nothing I can do about it now. After I finish this panel, a back panel, I'll knit the front panel and then the two sleeves... Auntie told me that I could finish it before the fall ended if I kept at it diligently.

"Mr. Park? That old writer guy? Oh my! You're still a baby, aren't you!" Auntie cried. She almost folded over from laughing as if I'd just said complete nonsense.

Still a baby? My mom gave birth to me when she was nineteen. All Auntie needs to do for me now is teach me how to knit. Who I like is none of her business.

I quietly opened the door. I can see that Auntie is busy washing *kimchi* ingredients in the kitchen. After I put on my slippers, I head out towards the bathroom in the corner, making my way carefully around the wall. I slowly turn on the water and splash my face as quick I can. I slip back into our room and close the door. Success! This proves that I'm almost a Seoulite.

"Someone as soft as you has to drink some Seoul water. That'll make you smarter," Mom said.

That was most likely why she sent me to Seoul.

철제 궤짝과 자개 경대 틈에 끼어놓은 내 여행가방을 잡아당겨서 비닐봉지를 꺼낸다. 아이섀도와 립스틱. 어제 아침 화장품 할인코너에서 새로 산 것이다. 아줌마가 보면 또 한마디 거들 것이다.

몇 번 썼다고 또 새 걸 사냐? 미친년.

시원한 바다 색깔의 아이섀도. 올 여름 유행색이 달라진 것을 난들 어쩌란 말인가.

나도 이젠 제법 화장하는 솜씨가 늘었다. 눈화장을 하면 다섯 살은 성숙해 보인다. 열여덟이면 결코 적은 나이가 아니다. 우리 엄마가 시집 간 나이가 열여덟이다. 새신랑 우리 아버지는 스무 살. 내가 올해 현수와 결혼을 한다면 우리가 딱 그 나이다. 그러나 나는 그 얘기를 절대로 현수에게 하지 않는다. 돌아가신 아버지야 그렇다 치더라도 엄마 나이가 좀 창피하다. 따지고 보면 내가 엉터리다. 엄마가 일찍 결혼한 것이 한편으로는 창피하면서도, 내 경우야 또 예외라고 생각하는 것이다. 이게 다 박 선생님 때문이다. 나이가 꽉 찬 박 선생님 처지로 보면 내가 올해라도 결혼 못할 것은 없다는 말이다.

비키니 옷장에서 새 스커트를 꺼내어 입는다. 지난주

My responsibility is to be a good waitress, but I don't have any obligations to help Auntie with the kitchen work.

I sit in front of the mother-of-pearl-inlaid lacquer dresser. Whenever I sit in front of this dresser with its red lacquer-stripped corners, I feel as if I am looking at Auntie's nails. Her manicure never lasts longer than a day. It's not surprising because she keeps her hands under water practically all day long. Still, she has a very sharp nose. Whenever Sister gets a manicure, Auntie immediately shows up and thrusts her fingernails out at her. Even if Sister tells her the color isn't right, that doesn't stop Auntie.

I pull my luggage out from the crack between the steel trunk and the lacquer dresser and remove a plastic bag from it. A case of eye shadow and a stick of lipstick. I bought them yesterday at a cosmetics discount store. Let Auntie have a look at them, and I know she won't miss the opportunity to make some sort of critique.

"How many times have you used the ones you bought before? Buying new ones again, you're crazy!" she'll say.

This is a blue eye shadow, though. Blue like the

35

휴일에 아줌마하고 동대문 시장에서 산 것이다. 아줌마 몰래 동네 수선집에서 치마길이를 오 센티 줄였다. 내가 이렇게 짧은 스커트를 입는 것을 알면 우리 엄마는 뭐라 하실까. 현수는 괜히 나만 보면 치마 길이를 가지고 한마디씩 한다. 그러나 내게는 짧은 게 어울린다.

골목 어귀 디피점 미스 양의 통다리라니. 현수는 괜히 내 앞에서 의식적으로 미스 양 얘기를 끄집어낸다. 얼굴이야 뭐 그렇다고 쳐도 그런 코끼리 다리를 상대로 내가 질투라도 해줄 것을 기대하는지. 다리통뿐만 아니다. 미스 양의 오리처럼 둥싯대는 히프. 그래도 자존심은 있어서, 미스 양은 곧 죽어도 큰소리다. 남자들은 실은 비쩍 마른 여자보다 살집 있는 여자를 좋아한다나. 나한테는 그렇게 말하면서 살 빼느라고 매일 점심을 굶는 사실이야 현수도 다 아는 일이다. 웃음소리는 어떻고? 제깐에는 애교라고 억지로 짜내는 그 이상한 웃음소리를 한번 들으면 웬만한 남자는 십 리 밖으로 도망쳐버릴 것이다.

계집이라카마 애교도 좀 있이야 되는 기고. 눈치 봐가미 배울 건 배워야 한다카이. 니야 체격도 니 아부지를

36

sea. What choice do I have but to buy a new one when the trend changes?

I'm quite skilled now when it comes to putting make-up on. After putting on a little eye make-up, I look five years older. Eighteen isn't too young. Mom married when she was eighteen. My father was twenty. If I marry Hyeon-su this year, we'd be the same kind of couple age-wise—but I never tell this to Hyeon-su. Father died, so he may not count. But I'm embarrassed by how young Mom is. Well, come to think of it, I'm ridiculous. Although I'm embarrassed by how young Mom was when she married, I feel I'll be fine marrying at my age. This is all because of Mr. Park. Since he's old enough, I just feel that I shouldn't rule out my marrying him this year.

I take out my new skirt from the plastic closet. I bought it when I went to Dongdaemun Market with Auntie during our off day. I had its length short-ened by five centimeters at a neighborhood altera-tion shop. I didn't tell Auntie about it, though. What would Mom say if she were to find out that I was wearing a skirt this short? Whenever Hyeon-su sees me, he comments on my skirt length, although it's none of his business. But, I look better in short

닮았으이.

언니와 엄마는 친 육촌간인데 그렇게 안 닮기도 어렵다. 언니는 키가 크고 바짝 마른 체격인 데 비해, 물질을 하는 엄마는 어깨가 벌어져 사내처럼 여문 체격이다. 긴 파마머리의 언니가 들에 핀 분홍색이나 자주색 엉겅퀴꽃을 닮았다면—프릴이 잔뜩 달린 자주색 니트 원피스를 입었을 때는 꼭 그렇다—엄마는 꽃과는 거리가 멀다. 사람이 아닌 물건으로 비기자면 절구나 옛날 풍구, 뭐 그런 덩치 큰 살림살이가 연상되곤 한다. 아버지만 돌아가시지 않았던들 엄마도 고생을 좀 덜하실 텐데. 현란한 화장에 주렁주렁 악세서리를 달고 나타난 언니를 보고, 목석 같은 엄마도 마음이 뒤숭숭했던 모양이다. 언니가 다녀간 날 밤, 장롱 서랍을 열고 밤새도록 이옷 저옷 걸쳐보며 한숨짓던 엄마 모습이 아직도 눈에 선하다.

나는 마라톤을 하기로 했어. 학교에서 선생님이 해보라고 해서. 황영조 선수도 해녀 아들이라서 가슴이 튼튼하다고 나도 한번 해보래. 중학교 가는 데 장학생으로 된다니까 나도 좋아. 누나도 좋지. 엄마도 내가 배 안

skirts.

Only, think of Miss Yang's thick legs, the girl working at the DP&E shop at the entrance of our alley! Hyeon-su makes sure to bring her up in front of me. I wonder how he can even expect me to be jealous of a girl with those elephant legs, let alone that plain face. It's not just her legs. There's her duck bottom, too! Still, being a proud girl, she doesn't get discouraged at all. She claims that men like plump girls more than thin ones. Even Hyeon-su knows that she secretly skips lunch everyday to lose weight after saying something like that in front of me. And her laugh! Most men would run far, far away, once they hear that strange wheezing sound she makes in an effort to be flirtatious.

"A girl should know how to make herself agreeable. You should try to learn certain things. You take after your father," Sister says.

Sister and Mom, though cousins, look so completely different from each other. Sister is tall and thin, while Mom, a diver, has broad, masculine shoulders. If Sister with her long wavy hair looks like a pink or purple thistle—especially when she wears a frilly, purple knit dress—then Mom just looks like she has nothing at all to do with flowers.

타니까 좋대.

영배는 국민학교 육학년치고는 편지도 야무지게 잘 쓴다. 엄마가 영배를 낳고 드러누워 있을 때 아버지 배가 돌아오지 않았으니, 아버지는 영배가 이세상으로 나온 줄도 모르고 저세상으로 들어가셨다. 그러니 영배가 아버지 얼굴을 기억할 리 없다. 나 역시…… 나는 사실 아버지 얼굴을 똑똑히 안다고 자부했었는데, 재작년에 엄마를 따라 두 재 넘어 외삼촌 장례식에 갔다가 외삼촌 영정을 보고 깜짝 놀랐다. 내가 아버지로 기억하고 있었던 얼굴이 바로 외삼촌 얼굴이었기 때문이었다. 집에 와서 엄마에게 채근을 하여 결혼사진을 들여다보니 아버지는 전혀 다른 얼굴이었다.

느그 아부지가 어데 외삼촌 닮았노, 택도 없지. 거무스름한 기나 닮았으까. 같이 배를 탔으이께네.

아버지 얼굴은 계집애처럼 눈, 코, 입술 모두 선이 가는 데 비해, 외삼촌은 코가 밤송이처럼 울퉁불퉁하게 붙어서 누가 보아도 우악스런 뱃사람 같았다. 그러니까 영배는 외탁을 한 셈이고 내 얼굴이 아버지를 닮은 것이다. 엄마가 들으면 섭섭하실지 모르지만, 나는 아버

If I compared her with an object, then she'd be something large like an old mortar or an old winnower. If only Father didn't pass away, then Mom wouldn't have had such a hard life. Even Mom, usually so unimpressionable, seemed upset when Sister showed up with her colorful make-up and many dangly accessories. I can still see how she sighed over and over again that night, taking and trying out various clothes from her closet.

"I decided to be a marathoner on my teacher's recommendation. He said that Hwang Young-cho had a strong heart because he was a diver's son and that I should try it, too. I like this idea because then I can go to middle school as a scholarship student. You like it, too, right? Mom likes it because I don't have to be a fisherman," Yeong-bae wrote.

Yeong-bae writes letters well for a sixth-grader. Father's boat never came back when Mom gave birth to Yeong-bae and so Father went to the other world without even knowing Yeong-bae was born. Naturally, Yeong-bae can't remember Father's face. I can't either, actually... In fact, I always thought that I remembered Father's face well, but I was surprised to see my maternal uncle's photo

지 쪽을 닮은 게 정말 다행이라고 생각한다. 딱 벌어진 어깨에 굵은 뼈마디, 두꺼운 입술까지 내가 닮았더라면 어쩔 뻔했을까.

「조금만 준비해요, 그깟 점심때 몇 명이나 온다구. 우리 먹을 거나 마련하면 되지.」

깜짝이야. 언니가 언제 왔는지 주방에서 아줌마와 말하는 소리가 들린다.

「그래도 당근이 없으니 색깔이 안 맞잖아? 야채 트럭 오는 것 기다리느니 슈퍼에 가서 얼른 사오는 게 낫겠어.」

주방장 아줌마의 말소리다.

「내가 갔다 올게요.」

나는 방문을 열고 신발을 꿰어 신으며 말한다.

「웬일이니, 심부름 한번 시키려면 생난리를 치는 계집애가.」

주인언니가 반색을 한다. 말이 끝나기도 전에 아줌마가 한마디 한다.

「심부름 핑계대고 나가서 또 언제나 들어오게?」

저 말솜씨하고는.

「그럼 아줌마가 직접 갔다 와요.」

when I attended his funeral after crossing over two hills with Mom two years ago. The face I remembered as Father's was, in fact, my uncle's. When I returned home, I asked Mom to show me their wedding photo. In that photo, Father's face was completely different from what I remembered.

"You think your father looks like your uncle? No no. They're both tanned, that's true. They were both fishermen," Mom said.

Father's face was delicate and had thin features— eyes, nose, lips, and all. My uncle, on the other hand, looked like a rough seaman with his chestnut burr nose. So, Yeong-bae takes after Mom and I take after Father. Mom might not be happy to hear this, but I'm glad that I take after my father's side. I can't even imagine myself with broad shoulders, thick joints, and thick lips.

"Please cook just a little. How many customers do we have at lunch anyway? Just cook for us," Sister said.

Goodness! I'm surprised to hear Sister talk with Auntie in the kitchen. I wonder when Sister showed up.

"Still, the color doesn't go very well without carrots, right? Instead of just waiting for the vegetable

「당근이나 들여놓고 싸돌아다니란 말여.」

나는 아줌마를 쌩하니 흘겨본다. 아줌마는 파를 썰면서 얼굴도 들지 않는다.

「얘, 너…… 치마 한번 멋있다?」

언니 눈이 쌩하니 내 종아리를 훑는다. 말은 안 해도 언니가 내 다리에 대해 열등감이 있는 것을 나는 벌써부터 알고 있다. 다리 하나만 비교한다면 언니보다 내가 낫고말고. 미스 장은 각선미가 만점이야. 다방의 단골 아저씨들이 내 다리를 만지려고 할 때는 소름이 끼치면서도 기분은 나쁘지 않다.

「뭐, 옛날부터 입던 건데.」

「옛날 거 좋아하시네. 시장 한번 가면 눈이 새빨개가지구 휘적거리고 다니는데…… 괜히 조심하라구. 콩꼬투리만한 년한테 님 뺏기고 울지 말구.」

아줌마가 키득대기 시작한다.

「……님이라니?」

언니가 눈이 둥그래져서 나와 아줌마를 번갈아 쳐다본다. 아줌마의 저 이죽거리는 심술보.

「아줌마는 알지도 못하면서 무슨 헛소리예요? 당근

44

truck, it'd be better just to run over to the super-market and buy some," said Auntie.

"I'll go," I say. I begin putting on my shoes.

"What's up? You always make such a fuss when I send you for errands," Sister says, her face brightening.

Even before Sister finishes her words, though, Auntie says, "I wonder when you'll be back? Doing errands is just an excuse."

Goodness. Just look at her talking. That's what I think, and I say, "You go, then, Auntie!"

"I mean, you should bring carrots first and then run around," says Auntie.

I give her a sidelong glance. But Auntie keeps chopping scallions and doesn't even bother to look up.

"Hey, you... I like that skirt!" Sister says.

Her eyes run across my legs. Although she never says it, I know that she's not happy about her legs. Of course, I have much prettier legs than she does. "Miss Chang has perfect legs!" Regulars at our shop sometimes try to touch my legs. I get goosebumps when they say this and reach over, but I feel flattered, too.

"Oh, I've had this for a long time."

얼마치나 사와요?」

나는 대답을 채 듣지 않고 주방을 빠져나온다. 아줌마의 커다란 목소리가 뒤따라온다.

「두 개만 사와. 중간치루. 싱싱한가 보구!」

다방 문을 나서서 계단을 내리닫는다. 언니한테 나는 더더욱 당당해질 필요가 있다. 사랑을 하려면 모든 것을 뛰어넘어야 한다. 용기와 인내가 아니고는 행복은 얻어낼 수 없는 것이다. 박 선생님에 대해서도 뺏든지 뺏기든지, 둘 중의 하나다. 전투 준비 완료!

2

「뭘 그렇게 골라? 겨우 두 뿌리 사간다면서.」

슈퍼 할머니가 눈을 흘긴다. 나이가 들었으니 눈 밑에 살주머니가 축 늘어진 건 어떻게 봐준다 쳐도, 말 한마디 곰살맞게 붙이지 못하는 이 할머니의 심보도 알아줘야 한다. 할머니 가게 물건들은 할머니랑 똑같이 늙었다. 먼지가 켜로 앉은 선물용 주스박스, 언제 받아놓은 것인지 알 수 없는 색 바랜 과자 봉지, 진열칸에 너저분

"Long time my ass! She's crazy looking for new clothes every time she goes to the market... Be careful! Don't lose your lover to a young girl and then cry about it later!" Auntie says, giggling.

"Lover?" Sister asks. Wide-eyed, she looks at Auntie and me. Auntie's so mischievous.

"What nonsense are you talking about, Auntie? How many carrots do you need?"

I leave the kitchen without waiting for her answer. Auntie's voice follows after me. "Just two. Mid-sized. Check if they are fresh!"

After leaving the coffee shop, I run down the stairs. I need to be more dignified in front of Sister. You have to overcome everything for love. You can't obtain happiness without courage and patience. Regarding Mr. Park, the choice is between the two—win him over or lose him forever. I'm ready to fight!

2

"Why are you so choosy? All you need is two carrots, right?" the granny at the mini-supermarket says, looking sideways at me. I can somehow feel generous towards her puffy eyes, because she's an

하게 꽂힌 두루마리 화장지들. 새로 들여놓는 야채라고
는 검은 보자기를 씌운 콩나물 한 통과 두부 몇 판 그리
고 쉬 상하지 않는 감자와 당근 박스가 고작이면서 할
머니는 툭하면 〈이 동네 것들은 늙은 거나 젊은 거나 얌
통머리가 없다〉며 투덜댄다. 골목 바깥, 새로 생긴 슈퍼
에 손님을 뺏기는 사실이 무척 약 오르는 모양이다.

「그만 헤적거리라니까! 멀쩡한 당근 다 상하겠네.」

「오래된 거 아녜요?」

「오늘 아침에 들여놨어. 물건 보면 몰라?」

할머니는 눈 깜짝도 않고 짜증을 낸다. 노인네가 의뭉
스럽기는. 당근 몸통이 이렇게 휘청거릴 정도면 받아놓
은 지 일주일은 실히 지났을 것이다. 하는 수 없다. 당근
두 뿌리 사자고 골목 밖에까지 가기도 그렇고. 그러고
보면 안경집 골목의 새댁 말이 백번 옳다. 〈할머니네 가
게 물건이 다른 집 것보다 훨씬 못하다. 게다가 값도 더
비싸며, 종류가 다양하지 못해서 어차피 큰 가게로 갈
수밖에 없다. 뭐니 뭐니 해도 물건을 동네사람들에게
강매하려는 그 마음가짐부터 고쳐 잡수셔야 한다……〉
등 조목조목 따지고 들었다는 말들이 다 맞는 얘기 아

old woman. But she really has a nasty temper, never saying anything nice to you. The stuff in her store is as old as her. Dust-covered gift juice box sets, faded plastic bags of expired candy, grubby-looking bathroom tissues poking out of display cases here and there. The only things new in this store are a few vegetables like the covered tub of bean sprouts, a few batches of tofu, and a boxful of potatoes and carrots, which can last for some time. Nevertheless, this granny grumbles all the time, "The old and the young in this neighborhood are shameless." She seems very upset because she's losing her customers to a new supermarket outside this alley.

"Stop rummaging! You're ruining my carrots."

"They're old, aren't they?"

"I got them this morning. Can't you just look at them?" She doesn't bat an eye when she spits this out. Sly old woman! Judging by the way these carrots have softened, they must have been there at least more than a week. I have no choice, though. I can't go so far as to the supermarket outside of this alley for just two carrots. Come to think of it, that bride at the eyeglass store alley was totally right when she told this granny:

닌가. 〈슈퍼에서 물건을 사들고 할머니 집 앞을 지날 때에 우리 맘이라고 편한 건 아니다. '이 할머니는 도대체 돌아가시지도 않네', 중얼거리게 만든 장본인이 바로 할머니 자신임을 명심하시라〉는 말은 좀 과하기는 했지만. 새댁과 할머니가 골목에서 실랑이하는 광경을 우연히 보게 된 삼층 신문보급소 소장 아저씨는 〈나이도 어린 여자가 안하무인〉이라고 혀를 내둘렀지만 하여간 할머니 행짜를 보면 그렇게 당해도 싸다는 생각이 든다.

할머니 손을 거쳐오면 백 원짜리 동전도 늙는다. 돈 내밀기가 무섭게 낚아채 배에 두른 전대에 쑤셔 넣으면서, 동전 몇 개 꺼내주는 데는 또 세고, 확인하고 오 분도 더 걸리는 것 같다. 우리 다방을 향해 뛰기 시작한다. 몇 집 떨어지지 않은 거리인데도 티셔츠가 비에 금방 젖어든다. 비야 오너라, 장마가 지면 어떠리. 나는 아무 곡조나 입에서 나오는 대로 흥얼거린다.

얘, 윤희야 여기…… 하는 주방 아줌마의 말을 뚝 분지른다. 방문을 열고 우산을 집어 들자마자 나는 튕기듯 밖으로 내닫는다. 튀어 오른 계단의 쇠편자는 밟을 때마다 꽹과리처럼 쨍쨍거린다.

"The stuff in your store is nowhere near as good as what's in other stores. Besides, your stuff is more expensive, and you have less selection. So, it's natural that we'd go to bigger stores. And more than anything else, you need to change your attitude. You're practically forcing your neighbors to buy your stuff..."

All her points were well said, each and every one of them. Of course, that bride went too far, when she said, "We don't feel good about it when we pass by your store, holding our bags from the supermarket. But just remember that you're the reason we say under our breath, 'I wonder why this granny hasn't died yet.'"

And, it's true that after accidentally seeing the bride and granny quarreling in the alley, the director uncle in charge of the newspaper delivery office on the third floor shook his head, saying, "That lady is too cocky." Still, from the way this granny behaves, I feel that she deserved that kind of treatment.

Passing through that granny's hand, sometimes it seems even a hundred *won* coin gets older. As soon as you hand her the money, she snatches it from your hand and stuffs it into her waist pouch.

부릉대는 지프가 보도에 고인 빗물을 튕기며 지나간다. 얼른 한쪽으로 비켜선다. 보슬비 오는 아침, 골목은 다시 한가롭다. 검은색 박쥐우산을 천천히 펼친다. 박 선생님의 손길이 남아 있는, 그의 체취가 배어 있는 우산. 사람의 감정이란 정말 묘하다. 미색의 플라스틱 손잡이가 달린 그의 박쥐우산이 내 손에 들어온 날부터 나는 비 오는 날이 무조건 좋아졌다. 언니 말대로 옥상의 빗물이 털보 아저씨네 지붕에 폭포처럼 떨어져서 거덜이 나거나 말거나.

우산을 어깨까지 나지막히 드리운다. 사르르 눈을 감는다. 그의 부드러운 팔이 내 어깨에 둘러지는 순간이다. 우산에 투덕대는 빗방울의 무게, 신선한 빗물 냄새. 그의 품에 안겨, 그의 흰 목덜미에 머리를 살포시 대고…… 촉촉한 초여름 공기가 이렇게 싱그러울 수가 없다.

열한 시까지만 돌아가면 다방 일은 걱정 없다. 매일 하는 홀 청소야 마음만 먹으면 이십 분으로 충분하다. 우산 건도 염려 없다. 박 선생님이 다방에 나타나는 때는 정오를 지나서다. 우산을 우리 방에 슬쩍 들여놓기

But when she has to give a few coins back, she counts them over and over again. It probably takes more than five minutes every time. I begin to run towards the coffee shop. Although it's only a few steps away, my T-shirt's quickly getting soaked. *Rain, rain! Who cares if it floods.* I hum a random tune that comes to the tip of my tongue.

"Hey, Yun-hi, here..." I don't stand around to wait for Auntie to finish her sentence. As soon as I open our room door and pick up an umbrella, I run out. The loosened pieces of iron on the edges of the stairs clang like a gong whenever I step on them.

A roaring jeep passes by, splashing rainwater pooled on the road. I step aside quickly. On this drizzly morning the alley becomes quiet again. I open my black umbrella slowly. An umbrella still with his touch, his body odor still lingering about it. A human feeling really is an intriguing thing. From the day I came by this plastic-handled umbrella of his, I started to taking to rainy days no matter what. I don't care whether the rain from our building crashes down and breaks the hairy uncle's roof or not, as Sister has said.

I lower the umbrella to my shoulders. I close my eyes slowly. It's in moments like these that I can

만 하면 되는 일이다. 어리숙한 박 선생님. 박 선생님은 자기 우산을 몰라볼지도 모른다. 그는 도대체 누가 자기를 좋아하고 있는지, 자기에게 어울리는 여자가 누군지도 도통 모른다. 그저 이세상에 언니밖에 없는 줄 알고…… 답답하기 짝이 없는 노릇이다. 칼국수만 해도 그렇다. 박 선생님은 칼국수를 무척 좋아한다. 거의 매일 칼국수를 먹으면서 질리지도 않는다. 언젠가 〈대통령도 칼국수를 좋아한다는데 한번 겨뤄보시라〉고 했더니, 박 선생님은 〈글쎄, 기회가 되면 그래도 좋고…… 바빠서 여기까지 오실 수 있을까〉 웃지도 않고 진지한 얼굴로 그렇게 대답하는 것이었다. 대통령과의 식사를 벌써 예전부터 벼르고 있었다는 식의 표정이었다. 그때는 어떻게, 웃을 수도 없어서 어물쩡 넘겨버리고 말았지만, 농담조차 심각하게 대답하는 박 선생님은 어찌 보면 머리가 모자라는 어린아이 같기도 하다.

우리 다방에서는 물론 커피나 음료를 팔지만, 점심때에는 간단한 칼국수와 김치볶음밥도 판다.

어차피 우리도 점심은 먹어야 하니까.

언니의 말이지만, 골목 안 이층의 다방 수입으로 그나

feel his arms gently around my shoulders. The slight weight of the raindrops pattering on the roof of my umbrella. Their fresh smell. In his arms, I lay my head back into his pale neck... The wet early summer air has never been fresher.

I don't have to worry about the coffee shop as long as I get back by eleven. I can finish cleaning the hall in twenty minutes if I want to. I've been doing it every day. I don't have to worry about the umbrella, either. Mr. Park comes to the coffee shop past noon. All I have to do is to tiptoe back and return the umbrella to our room. So clueless that Mr. Park! Maybe he doesn't even recognize his own umbrella. He doesn't have a clue who likes him, or which woman would truly make him happy. He just thinks Sister is the only woman for him in this world... It's so irritating.

It's true of the chopped noodles and Mr. Park, too. Mr. Park likes chopped noodles a lot. He eats them almost every day, never getting tired of them. Sometime ago, when I told him, "I heard that our president likes chopped noodles, too. Why don't you compete with him and see who likes them better?" he answered in an absolutely serious sort of tone, "Well, maybe, if there was a chance... but

마 살림이 꾸려지는 데에는 점심식사로 들어오는 수입도 무시할 수 없다. 주방 아줌마가 때로 통박을 부리기는 하지만 그 일을 전담하고 있다. 언니는 그 때문에 아줌마에게 무척 고마워한다. 점심식사를 팔자는 제안도 주방 아줌마가 했다는 것이다. 아줌마는, 언니 말을 빌리면 한마디로 진국이다. 주방에 들어가 봐도 단무지 한 조각, 나물 한 젓가락, 허투루 버리는 법이 없다. 뒤통맞은 말씨와 찌부러진 눈이 흠이기는 하지만 속내는 무척 따뜻한 사람이다.

엄마보다도 열 살이나 위인 아줌마는 내 생각도 꽤 살뜰히 해주는 편이다. 보통 자정이 넘어서, 다방 영업이 마무리된 다음에나 잠자리에 드는 나는 아침 아홉 시 정도까지 잘 수밖에 없다. 밤 열 시께에 잠이 들어 여섯 시쯤 일어나는 아줌마는 내 잠을 깨울까봐 무척 조심한다. 조용조용히 요를 갠 후 주방에 나가서도, 설거지나 도마질처럼 시끄러운 일은 되도록 삼가는 것을 말은 안 해도 내가 다 알고 있다. 그놈의 찌부러진 눈만 아니라면, 아줌마의 얼굴도 그리 밉상은 아닌 편이다. 피부도 하야니 고운 편이고 콧날이나 턱의 선도 그런 대

do you really think he'd come here? He must be so busy."

He looked as if he's been waiting all this while to have this kind of opportunity with the president of our country. Since I couldn't really laugh right there, I just let it go. But considering Mr. Park even takes jokes like this seriously, he really is kinda like a stupid child.

We don't only sell coffee and other drinks in our coffee shop, but also simple dishes like chopped noodles and *kimchi* fried rice during lunchtime.

"We have to eat lunch ourselves, too, you know," Sister says.

At any rate, the income from lunch is an important contribution to Sister's coffee shop business. Since we're located on the second floor in an alley, her revenue from the coffee sales isn't enough. Auntie takes charge of lunch, although sometimes she can be difficult. Sister is very appreciative of her contributions. In fact, I heard that it was Auntie herself who proposed the idea of selling lunch. Auntie's the real thing, according to Sister. When you enter the kitchen, you know she's not throwing away even a single slice of pickled radish or a chopstick's worth of a vegetable side. Despite her

로 깨끗하게 빠졌다. 눈만 아니라면…… 아줌마는 정
말 소박맞을 이유가 없다.

아줌마 눈은 왼쪽이 씰그러져 있다. 눈꺼풀이 불에 덴
듯 말려 올라가 왼쪽 눈알이 그대로 떨어질 듯 생급스
럽다. 날 때부터 그런 건지, 어떻게 하다 다친 건지 도대
체 알 수 없다. 새살맞은 언니도 아줌마하고 햇수로 4년
째라는데 아직껏 그 일에 대해서는 잘 모른다. 눈 애기
만 나오면 아줌마가 미친 듯이 소리치며 화를 내기 때
문이다. 남편이 무슨 짓을 해서 그녀를 그 꼴로 만들어
놓았거나, 아니면 그 씰그러진 눈에 만정이 떨어져 아
줌마를 소박 놓았거나다. 서울에 처음 올라와서 나는
주방장 아줌마의 눈을 보고 잔뜩 겁을 먹었었다. 웃지
도 않고 자꾸 고개를 외로 꼬면서 나를 살피는 모습이,
동화에 나오는 마귀할멈이 바로 그런 모습일 것 같았
다. 아줌마의 말려 올라간 왼쪽 눈은 잘 때에도 뜨고 자
는 것일까, 나는 그게 무척 궁금했다. 며칠이 지나 우연
히 아줌마의 자는 모습을 보게 되었는데 다행히 눈이
감기기는 감겼다. 오른쪽 눈처럼 똑바로 감기지 않고
많이 씰그러져서 감기긴 했지만, 하여간 두 눈이 다 감

brutal candor and hard looks, she really is warm at heart.

Auntie is ten years older than Mom and is pretty caring towards me, too. I usually go to bed after midnight when we finish our day's work. So I have to sleep until around nine in the morning. Auntie goes to bed around ten at night and gets up at around six in the morning. So she's always very careful not to wake me up. She folds her mattress and comforter almost without making a sound. And although she doesn't tell me, I know she tries to avoid doing noisy things in the kitchen like doing the dishes or chopping vegetables. If not for her evil eye, her face wouldn't look so bad. Her skin is pale and smooth. Her nose and chin lines are on the cleaner side. But that eye... her husband really wouldn't have had any reason to treat her the way he did.

Her left eye is crooked. Her left eyelid is rolled up like it was burned, so her left eye bulges out suddenly at times. It looks as if it might pop out at any moment. I have no idea if she was born with it, or if she got hurt. Even Sister, who's really sociable and would've found out these sort of things, doesn't know, either, although she's been working with

겨서 잠든 것을 보니 마음이 놓였다.

아줌마는 보통때는 무척 사람이 좋은데 화가 났다 하면 사흘은 간다. 애꿎은 주방의 그릇들이 우당탕탕 몸살을 한다. 언니 말을 들으면 아줌마 남편은 새 여자와 살림을 차렸다고 한다. 새 여자와의 사이에 꽤 장성한 아들도 둘이라고 한다. 〈웬수, 썩어빠진 인간, 마누라 등쳐먹고 사는 아귀 같은 남정네.〉 입에서 나오는 대로 별 말을 다하면서도, 월말이면 월수 이자받듯 다방에 들어서는 남편에게 아줌마는 생활비를 꼬박꼬박 건네준다. 나보고는 돈을 어떻게든 모아라, 한 푼이라도 낭비하면 안 된다,있는 잔소리를 다해 대면서 정작 아줌마는 월급을 거의 고스란히 남편에게 털리는 것이다.

밀대로 밀어놓은 듯 납작한 얼굴의 아저씨는 돈을 받는 순간에도 아줌마를 정면으로 쳐다보지 않는다. 아줌마 역시 옆으로 서서 잘 쳐다보지도 못하고 비죽이 봉투만 내민다. 〈몸 편하나?〉 하면 〈매 그렇지요〉 한다. 기껏해야 자기 아들 안부 한두 마디 건네다 남편이 돌아가고 나면, 아줌마는 방으로 들어가 벽을 보고 눕는다. 그러고는 또 어느새 한 달, 아줌마가 웬일로 뽀얗게 분

Auntie for almost four years now.

It's because Auntie goes absolutely berserk whenever anybody brings up the subject of her left eye. It's most likely either that her husband did something terrible to hurt her or that she was kicked to the curb by her husband because of that awful eye.

When I first came to Seoul, I was terrified of her because of that eye. She never smiled and kept looking at me sideways. I thought that this must be exactly how the witch in folktales looked. Did she sleep with that rolled-up eyelid open? I got so curious about it. I happened to see her sleep one night and found out that fortunately she did close that eye. Although it wasn't closed quite like her right eye, I still felt better after seeing her sleep with both eyes closed.

Auntie is usually a good-natured person. But once she gets angry, her anger lasts at least three days. Innocent plates and bowls suffer; they crash and rattle when she goes off. According to Sister, Auntie's husband lives with another woman. He even has two grown sons with this new woman. Auntie curses him viciously

"My arch enemy, a rotten brute, a devil of a hu-

을 발랐다든지 까닭 없이 잦은 기침을 하는 듯하면 영락없이 남편이 오는 날인 것이다.

기분이 좋으면 아줌마는 〈사랑은 눈물의 씨앗〉이라는 노래를 흥얼거린다. 그러고는 이 집엔 처녀만 셋이라고 너스레를 떤다. 언니도 호적으로는 시집간 적이 없으니 처녀이고, 아줌마 역시 자기가 본처이기는 하지만 혼인 사실을 올리지 않아서 호적상으로는 처녀라고 한다. 〈호적에 올리지도 않았다면서 어떻게 본처일 수 있어요?〉 하면, 〈정식으로 사주단자를 받았으니까〉 하고 딱 부러지게 대답한다. 나는 아줌마의 행동을 이해할 수가 없다. 나는 적어도 그렇게는 안 산다. 아무리 본처로 인정해준다 해도, 딴 여자와 사는 남자를 평생 남편으로 믿고 섬기는 따위 웃기는 짓은 절대 안 한다. 열녀문 세울 일 있나, 지금이 어떤 세상이라고.

「아침부터 어딜 싸돌아다니냐?」

누군가가 우산을 버쩍 쳐든다. 현수다. 오토바이에 앉은 채 우장을 걸친 품새가, 신문 배달이 빠진 집에 신문을 가져다주고 오는 길인 모양이다.

「무슨 상관이람?」

man being, freeloader, racketeer living off his wife..." she says.

Still, she never misses dispensing his allowance every month when he shows up like a creditor dropping by the coffee shop to collect his monthly interest. Auntie nags me whenever she has the chance, "You should save money no matter what" or "Don't waste even a cent!" But Auntie allows her husband to rob her of almost her entire monthly salary whenever he drops by.

Her husband has a flat face, as flat as if it was flattened by a roller. He doesn't look her straight in the eye, even at the moment when he receives the money from her. Auntie, in turn, stands aside and pushes the envelope towards him, looking away. When he asks, "Are you doing okay?" she answers, "I'm doing the same as usual." When he leaves after saying, at most, a few words about his own sons, she goes to our room and lies down, and faces straight against the wall. Then, a month later, a day comes when she suddenly powders her face or begins to cough frequently for no reason. That's the day when her husband comes.

When Auntie's in a good mood, she hums the song, "Love is the Seed of Tears." Then she says

나는 그에게 소리를 지른다. 어떻담? 하는 식의 말투는 언니에게 배운 말이다. 언니 역시 경상도라, 배운 서울말일 텐데도 그런 말투는 정말 앙증맞다. 나는 그대로 걸음을 빨리한다. 현수가 오토바이를 두 손으로 끌며 허겁지겁 따라온다. 뭐, 기분이 나쁘지는 않다. 현수따위 풋내 나는 친구, 나는 관심도 없지만, 자기로서야 나를 따라오는 게 당연하고말고. 미스 양이 이 꼴을 봐야 하는데. 골목 입구 미스 양네 디피점까지는 아직도 더 가야 한다. 그녀는 현수가 나한테 이렇게 추근댄다는 사실을 까맣게 모른다.

「어디 가? 태워다줄까?」

「됐네.」

「이번 노는 날 어때?」

그가 다그친다. 휴일에 자기 오토바이를 타고 야외로 놀러가자는 이야기를 벌써 몇 번이나 했었다.

현수가 가진 오토바이는 새것이다. 그리고 자기 것이다. 두어 달 전까지만 해도 그가 몰던 신문보급소 소유의 오토바이는 그야말로 길에 내놓아도 가져가는 사람만 골치 아플 구닥다리 고물이었다. 모양도 삼십 년은

nonsense like, "There are three virgins living in this house." According to her, Sister has never been married, so she's a virgin, and Auntie herself is also a virgin because she, the true wife, was never legally registered as her husband's wife. If I ask her, "So if you're not legally registered as his wife, how could you be his true wife?" she answers firmly, "Because I'm the one who received the formal letter to the house of the fiancée where the four pillars of the bridegroom-to-be are written."

I can't understand the way she lives. At the very least, I won't live like her. No matter how true a wife I might be recognized as, I won't waste my entire life serving a husband who lives with another woman. That's nonsense. I won't need to have the Gate of a Faithful Wife erected for me like I'm living during the Chosŏn dynasty.

Suddenly I hear a voice say, "Where are you running to this early in the morning?" A man raises his umbrella. It's Hyeon-su. Judging by the way he's riding his motorcycle and wearing his raincoat, he must be on his way back from a delivery to a house he missed during his early morning rounds.

"None of your business!" I yell at him. I learned to finish my sentences this way from my Sister. She

되어 보이는 구식인데다가 페인트를 덧칠하여 누덕누덕한 꼴은 어찌하고라도, 시동이 걸리지 않아 애를 먹었다. 한번 신문 배달을 나갈 때마다 삼십 분은 부릉거리니 동네 가게마다 한마디씩 거들곤 했다. 슈퍼 할머니 역시 〈시동 걸 시간 있으면 그 다리로 벌써 뛰어갔다 왔겠다〉고 고래고래 소리를 질러대고, 순해빠진 표구집 털보 아저씨조차, 시동 거는 소리를 듣다못해 〈어이, 내 자전거로 신문 갖다 주고 오지〉 했다. 그때 나는 왜 그리 웃음이 나던지. 이층에서 내려다보면서 깔깔거리던 내 웃음소리를 현수가 들었다. 나를 올려다보던 그의 얼굴, 새빨개지다 못해 파란색으로 변하며 곧 울음을 터뜨릴 것 같은 표정이었다. 나는 얼른 고개를 들이밀고 창문을 닫아버렸다. 지금 생각해도 그 일은 좀 미안하다.

그리고 보름이나 지났을까, 그는 새 오토바이를 타고 나타났다. 그가 거드름을 피우던 꼴이라니. 건물 앞에 오토바이를 내놓고 하루 종일 먼지를 닦더니, 시험해본답시고 경적을 자꾸 울리는 것이었다. 신문사 측에서 중고품을 사주려 하는 것을 새 오토바이를 사주지 않으

must have picked up this intonation in Seoul as she's really from Gyeongsang-do. It's cute. I keep walking fast. Hyeon-su also walks his motorcycle quickly, holding it with both of his hands. Well, I don't feel really offended, though. A greenhorn like Hyeon-su. Although I'm not interested in him, it's natural enough for him to follow me around. Miss Yang should see this. We have some distance to the ally entrance DP&E shop. She has no idea that Hyeon-su practically stalks me like this.

"Where are you going? You wanna ride?"

"I'm fine."

"What do you say about this coming holiday?" he asks.

He's been bugging me for a while, asking me to go on a picnic with him on his motorcycle during the coming holiday.

Hyeon-su's motorcycle is new, and it's his. The motorcycle, which he rode until a few months ago, belonged to the newspaper delivery office. It was so old that it would have been more of a headache than anything if someone came along and stole it off the street. It looked old-fashioned, probably thirty years old. Not only that, it looked practically patchwork because it had been painted over and

면 〈그만 두겠다〉고 자기가 말했더니 결국 새것으로 바꿔주었다는 것이다.

까짓 것, 오토바이 한 대 얼마 된다구. 차도 아닌데. 신문 배달 하려면 사실 신문사 이미지도 있는 것 아니냐구요?

그가 떵떵거린 내용은 사실과는 좀 달랐다. 보급소 소장 아저씨 말로는 신문사에서 현수에게 사준 것이 아니라, 현수가 앞으로 일 년 동안 나올 네 번의 보너스를 포기하고 월부로 새것을 샀다는 것이었다. 주방 아줌마는 현수가 헛똑똑이라고 한참 흉을 보았지만, 나는 그 일만은 현수가 잘했다고 생각한다. 사람이 자존심이 있지 헌 오토바이는 정말 너무했다. 젊은 애가 기분 문제 아니냐 말이다.

「같이 갈 여자 많잖아?」

나는 목소리를 착 깔며 부드럽게 대꾸한다. 현수가 내 애인이 아니라도, 그에게 일부러 점수를 잃을 필요는 없으니까.

「야야, 내가 뭐 상대가 없어서 그러는 줄 아냐? 네가 휴일에도 밖에 나가지도 못하고 할망구들 새에 볶이는

over again. Besides, it wouldn't start easily; it gave Hyeon-su a hard time all the time. Whenever Hyeon-su had to leave for delivery, it needed to be revved up for thirty minutes before starting.

People from all other stores in the alley would complain about it. The mini-super granny yelled, "During all this time you've wasted starting that motorcycle you could have just run and already made your deliveries and come back."

Even the hairy uncle at the frame shop got tired of all the noise and said, "Hey, why don't you use my bicycle?"

I wondered why I laughed so hard at the time? Hyeon-su heard me giggle from the second floor. When he looked up at me, his face was so flushed it was almost purple. And he looked like he was about to burst into tears. I quickly shrank from the window and closed it. I feel bad about this even now.

Probably about a fortnight after that incident, he showed up with a new motorcycle one day. My, how he came swaggering in that day! After parking it in front of our building, he spent the whole day dusting it. He also kept honking his new horn. His excuse was that he was testing it. According to

게 안돼서 그러지.」

하여간 틈을 주면 안 된다. 좀 사정을 봐주려니까 그
새에 까불기 시작한다.

「봐줘서 눈물 나네.」

나는 시틋하게 대답하고는 걸음을 재촉한다.

「의정부 쪽으로 달리면 길이 얼마나 좋은데. 경치도
끝내주고. 야, 너 도대체 어디 가는데 이렇게 바뻐?」

현수가 우산대를 잡는다. 순간 기분이 묘하다. 박 선
생님의 우산, 우산대를 거머잡은 현수의 손. 두 남자가
서로 대결하는 듯한 분위기. 내게 화냥기가 있는 것일
까. 기분이 나쁘지만은 않다. 그의 덜퍽진 손도 그리 싫
지는 않다. 사내는 패기가 있어야 한다. 힘도 좀 세고.
그의 풋풋한 땀냄새도 괜찮다. 그러나…… 내 마음속
에는 박 선생님 하나뿐이다. 단지 나는 누구든지, 설사
내가 상대방을 차버리는 한이 있더라도, 다른 사람이
나를 싫다고 하는 것은 못 참는다.

「되게 비싸게 구네. 그럼 극장에나 가든지?」

저만치 골목 어귀, 휘우듬하게 자리잡은 미스 양네 가
게의 〈필름〉이라고 씌어진 붉은 깃발이 보이기 시작한

him, he got it from the newspaper company after insisting that he needed a new one. When the company offered to exchange the old one with another used motorcycle, he threatened to quit unless they gave him a new motorcycle.

"My, how expensive can a motorcycle get? It's not a car, right? Shouldn't you also have to consider the newspaper's image, too?"

That was Hyeon-su's version, but the truth was a little different. According to the delivery office director, it wasn't the newspaper company that had bought it for Hyeon-su. The truth of the matter was that Hyeon-su had given up the quarterly bonuses he was going to get for the next year and had bought the motorcycle on monthly installments. Although Auntie made a fuss about it for a while, calling Hyeon-su a gasbag, I thought Hyeon-su was smart to get it. For a proud person, a used motorcycle is unacceptable. It's a matter of morale for a young man.

"I bet you already have a whole bunch of girls lined up to go with you, don't you?" I say, lowly and softly. I don't have to piss him off intentionally, although he's not my boyfriend.

"Hey, do you think I'm taking you because I have

다. 나는 갑자기 조바심이 난다. 현수가 더 이상 따라오지 않고 걸음을 멈추었기 때문이다. 미스 양네 가게 앞이 차마 못 건널 바다라도 되나? 나쁜 자식, 약아빠지기는. 치사하게 양다리를 걸치고.

「극장 못 가서 안달 난 사람들끼리나 가시지!」

미스 양이 들었을까. 나는 일부러 크게 소리치고는 종종걸음을 친다. 어디다 나를 비교하느냐 말이다. 천하의 둔치. 내 가치를 모른다면 그것도 현수, 제 팔자다. 싸구려 애들은 싸구려 애들끼리 어울릴 수밖에. 미스 양에게서 〈현수가 가끔 디피점에 들러 차를 마시고 간다〉는 말을 들었을 때 나는 다 알아봤다.

「눈에 시퍼렇게 그게 뭐냐? 천박하게!」

깜짝이야. 등 뒤에서 소리 지르는 그의 고함에, 나는 나도 모르게 그 자리에 우뚝 서버린다. 얼굴에 갑자기 열이 확 오른다. 지나가던 아줌마가 내 얼굴을 똑바로 쳐다본다. 우산을 폭 내려 얼굴을 가린다. 우산이 없었더라면 어쩔 뻔했을까. 오토바이 시동 거는 소리. 이내 부웅 멀어져간다. 저 자식을 그냥. 나는 여기저기 고인 물웅덩이를 건너뛰기 시작한다. 미스 양네 〈필름〉 깃발

nobody else to take? It's because I feel sorry for you because you can't go out on a holiday and because you're bothered by grannies all the time."

My, you just couldn't let your guard down with him. I try to be nice to him, and he walks all over me.

"I'm so moved," I answer, and narrow my eyes and quicken my steps.

"Do you know how nice it is to take ride out to Euijeongbu? The scenery's incredible, too! Hey, where are you going? Why are you so busy all of a sudden?"

Hyeon-su grabs at my umbrella handle. I feel a little strange. Mr. Park's umbrella, and Hyeon-su's hand grabbing at its handle. It feels as if the two men are confronting each other over me. Am I being a little promiscuous? I don't feel too bad about it. I don't dislike Hyeon-su's large hand. A man should be bold. And he should be strong, too. I like the strong odor of his body, too. Still... the only man I have room for in my heart is Mr. Park. However, I can't stand the thought of someone disliking me, even if he is someone I'll end up dumping later.

"You really think you're something, huh! Do you

이 휙 지나간다. 어린애들은 가라, 가라. 하여간 현수, 쟤는 무식해서 안 된다.

횡단보도를 건너 마로니에 공원으로 들어선다. 젊은 남녀들로 벅적대던 벤치는 물론, 밤늦게까지 노래가 그치지 않는 악사 무대에도 빗물이 흥건히 고였을 뿐 인적이라곤 없다. 저만치, 한 우산을 쓰고 걸어가는 연인 한 쌍이 보인다. 여자가 자신의 우산은 접어들고 남자의 팔짱을 끼었다. 여자는 긴 생머리에다 노란 바바리를 걸쳤다. 비 오는 날에는 노랑이 참 상큼해 보인다. 나도 모르게 한숨이 나온다. 그렇지만 나도 혼자는 아니다. 박 선생님이 이렇게 큼지막한 우산으로 내리는 비를 막아주고 있지 않은가.

일도, 내 이름은 일도야. 길이 하나뿐이라는 거지.

왠지 빗줄기 같은 박 선생님. 그의 목소리가 촉촉히 내 몸을 휘감는다. 우산을 최대한으로 폭 내려쓴다. 어깻죽지에 우산살이 배겨서 아프기까지 하다.

내가 요새 상상하고 있는 장면은 바로 이 공원에서의 일이다. 우연히 공원에 들른 박 선생님과 마주치는 것이다. 나는 깜짝 놀라 발을 멈춘다. 박 선생님의 핏기 없

wanna see a movie, then?"

I catch a glimpse of the red flag with the word, "film," on it sticking out from Miss Yang's DP&E shop far away at the slight bend near the alley entrance. I suddenly feel anxious, because Hyeon-su's stopped following me. Is the street in front of Miss Yang's shop a sea that you can't cross? Bastard! How sly of him! How disgraceful! He's playing both of us.

"Why don't you go with someone who can't wait to go to the movie theater like you?"

I wonder if Miss Yang heard me. I shout as loudly as I can on purpose and then I begin to walk fast. How dare he compare me with her? The dumbest man in the world! If he can't appreciate my true worth, that's his problem. A cheapo is attracted to another cheapo. That's expected. When Miss Yang told me, "Hyeon-su sometimes drops by the DP&E shop for a tea," I immediately knew it was the truth.

"What's with all that blue on your eyelids? It looks cheap!" Hyeon-su yells at me from behind.

I'm shocked. I stand still, rooted to the spot. My face suddenly turns a bright red. A passerby auntie looks straight at me. I lower the umbrella to hide my face. Thank goodness that I have this umbrella!

는 얼굴에 반가운 웃음이 퍼진다.

윤희씨, 내가 술 한잔 살까.

나는 다소곳이 그의 뒤를 따른다. 그가 잘 들르는 포
장마차다. 그는 아무 말 없이 소주를 몇 잔 들이켠다.

그만 드세요, 몸에 안 좋잖아요.

걱정이 되어 한마디 하면 박 선생님이 정겹게 웃는다.

……윤희씨는 시집가면 남편 사랑을 듬뿍 받을 거야.

그리고 또다시 술을 마신다. 해야 할 말을 꺼내지 못
하고 고민하는 눈치가 역력하다. 내가 먼저 운을 뗀다.

왜 결혼하지 않으세요?

윤희씨는…… 내가 결혼하자고 하면 할래?

그야…… 박 선생님이 원하신다면요.

그는 아무 말 없이 다시 술을 따른다. 내가 말리려고
술병을 잡는다. 그의 손이 내 손을 덥석 잡는다. 그러고
는 나를 와락 껴안는다. 그의 억센 팔 힘에 나는 꼼짝 못
하고 그의 품에 안긴다…….

이건 아니다. 박 선생님이 내게 이럴 분이 아니다. 언
니에게라면 몰라도. 나 같은 것은 안중에도 없다. 갑자
기 서글픈 생각이 든다. 짝사랑.

I hear the sound of a motorcycle starting. Then, it roars away. That bastard! I begin to jump over puddles here and there. I quickly pass by the "film" flag of Miss Yang's shop. Go away, you children! Anyway, Hyeon-su is too ignorant.

I cross the street and enter Marronnier Park. There's nobody around. There are puddles all over, not only on the benches that are usually crowded with young couples but also on the concert stage where musicians sometimes perform until very late at night. I can see a couple walking away under an umbrella some distance away. The girl is carrying her folded umbrella in one hand and links her arm with the man's. Her hair is long and naturally straight, and she is wearing a yellow raincoat. On a rainy day, yellow looks very fresh. I sigh unconsciously. Still, I'm not alone, either. Isn't Mr. Park and his big umbrella here to cover me and protect me from rain?

"Il-do, my name is Il-do. It means a single road," he'd said.

Somehow, he feels like streaks of rain. His wet voice envelops me. I lower the umbrella as low as possible. It hurts when I rest it upon my shoulders because the umbrella ribs jab my shoulder blades.

이런 상상은 어떨까. 술에 잔뜩 취한 박 선생님이 다 방에 나타난다. 언니가 보는 앞에서 〈윤희, 나하고 어디 좀 갈까〉. 빌어먹을. 왜 나는 술기운 없는 맨 정신의 박 선생님, 언니와 전혀 별개인 남자로서의 박 선생님을 상상할 수 없는 것일까.

자정이 지나 다방 문을 닫으려면 언니는 대개 술이 취해 있다. 언니는 거리낌 없이, 같이 술을 마신 남자와 부둥켜안은 채로 다방을 나서곤 한다. 순진한 박 선생 님은 아무것도 모른다. 야간학원 강의 때문에 항상 오 후 다섯 시경에 돌아가기 때문이다. 주방 아줌마도 웃 긴다. 내가 언니의 행동거지에 대해서 입바른 소리라도 할라치면 벌컥 화를 낸다. 언니가 어떻게 살든 상관 말 라는 이야기다. 언니처럼 불쌍한 여자도 없다나. 그런 일은 전혀 모르는 척, 특히 박 선생님 앞에서는 입 뻥긋 도 말라고 몇 번씩 단도리를 하는 것이다.

왜, 박 선생님하고 결혼 안 해요?

두어 달 전이던가, 민방위 훈련을 하는 시각이었다. 홀에 손님이라곤 아무도 없고 언니와 주방 아줌마, 나 셋이 앉았을 때 내가 언니에게 물었었다. 언니가 피식

These days, I like to imagine this scene in the park. In my mind, I run into Mr. Park here. Surprised, I freeze. A smile begins to spread over Mr. Park's pale face; he is glad to see me.

"Yun-hi, shall I buy you a drink?"

I follow after him without a word. We go to a covered cart bar, Mr. Park's favorite hangout. He downs a few cups of *soju* without saying a word.

"Please stop drinking. It isn't good for your health."

After I say this, my voice clearly full of worry, he smiles at me affectionately.

"Your husband will love you dearly, Yun-hi," he says, after a slight pause.

Then, he takes another shot. I can tell he wants to say something, but can't muster up courage.

I ask him, "Why don't you get married?"

"Would you marry me... if I proposed?"

"Of course... if you wanted to."

He pours *soju* again without responding. I grab the *soju* bottle before he can finish. In response, he clutches my hand. Then, he suddenly pulls me into his arms. I can't help being caught up in his embrace.

This won't do, though. Mr. Park wouldn't do that

웃으며 대답했다.

그 샌님은 나하고 결혼하고 싶어 하지 않아. 그저 동정하는 거지. 왜 있잖아, 싸구려.

박 선생님은 언니만 좋아하잖아요.

날 좋아하는 게 아니라니까. 차마 내 곁을 떠나지 못하는 자기 자신을 좋아하는 거지. 그런 면에서는 미선씨도 마찬가지고. 내가 불쌍해 뵈는가봐. 윤희야, 너두 내가 불쌍해 뵈니?

언니가 깔깔거렸다.

미선씨는 가끔 언니에게 전화를 한다. 전화가 왔다 하면 언니는 만사를 제쳐놓고 한 시간이 넘도록 떠들어대곤 한다. 미선씨가 박 선생님의 연인이었다는 사실이 웃긴다. 한때 연적이었던 여자끼리, 그것도 미선씨가 딴 남자와 결혼한 후에 먼저 언니에게 전화를 걸었다는 사실이 또한 웃긴다.

언니와 주방 아줌마의 말을 종합해보면, 언니는 고등학교 2학년 때 집을 나와 서울행 기차를 탔다고 했다. 사창가에 팔려가, 사내를 받은 지 며칠 안 되어 만난, 휴가 나왔던 군인이 바로 박 선생님이라는 것이다. 손가

80

to me, although he might to Sister. He doesn't even notice me. Suddenly, I feel sad. Unrequited love.

How about this scene? Mr. Park shows up in the coffee shop, completely drunk. In front of Sister, he says to me, "Yun-hi, shall we go somewhere?" Shit! Why can't I imagine him sober? Or as a man who has nothing to do with Sister?

Past midnight, around the time we close the coffee shop, Sister is usually drunk. Most of the times, she shamelessly goes out with a man that she eventually gets drunk with. Poor naïve Mr. Park does not know about it at all. He always leaves our coffee shop around 5 PM to teach at a cram school at night. Auntie is ridiculous, too. If I criticize Sister for her conduct, Auntie gets mad at me. She tells me I shouldn't meddle with the way Sister lives. Nobody has it as bad as Sister, huh? Auntie tells me that I should never talk about Sister's conduct in front of Mr. Park, that I should pretend to know nothing at all about it.

"Why don't you marry Mr. Park?" I asked one day a few months ago during Civil Defense training. There were only the three of us in the hall, Sister, Auntie, and me.

Sister grinned and said, "That gentleman scholar

락 하나 건드리지 않고 꼬박 밤을 지새고 이튿날 돌아간 그는, 그날 오후 다시 그 집에 나타났다고 한다. 포주에게 고래고래 소리를 지르며 언니를 내놓으라고 떼를 썼다. 박 선생님은 늘씬하게 얻어맞은 채 내쫓겼고 언니는 그날 밤으로 다른 집으로 옮겨지고. 그리고 2년 후 언니는 길에서 우연히 박 선생님과 마주쳤다는 것이다.

그러니까 내가 청량리 앞 룸살롱에 있을 때였지…….나보고 정식으로 사과하는 거야. 내 문제를 해결해주지 못하고 그때 그냥 귀대해서 정말 미안하다나. 웃기지 않니? 어떻게 해결해줘? 나는 그 샌님에게 기대도 안했었어. 처음 만났을 때에야, 내 하는 짓이 워낙 서투르고, 그냥 밤새, 무슨 말이건 하라니까, 억지로 사창가에 붙들려왔다고 살려달라고 했을 뿐이지. 나야 집에서 나와 서울에 올라올 때부터 각오하고 있었는데 뭘.

룸살롱에 샌님이 자꾸 찾아오는데…… 뭐, 분위기 맞춰줬지. 찔찔 짜기도 하고. 어떡허니? 자꾸 나보고 미안하다는데. 아르바이트했다고 목돈도 쥐어주더라. 마담한테 빚을 갚으라나. 웃기는 일이지. 나는 처음부터 빚이라곤 없었어. 당당하게 요구했었지, 나눠먹자고. 내

doesn't want to marry me. He just pities me. It's just cheap pity."

"Mr. Park only likes you, though."

"He doesn't like me. He likes himself. He likes the image of himself as the kind of person who would choose never to leave me. Mi-seon's like that, too. I must look pitiful to them. Yun-hi, do you think I'm pitiful, too?" Sister said. She giggled.

Mi-seon occasionally calls Sister. When Mi-seon calls, Sister drops everything then and there and chats with her for over an hour. It's funny because Mi-seon used to be Mr. Park's girlfriend. Former love rivals calling each other, now that's funny. Also the fact that Mi-seon, after marrying another man, initiates these calls to Sister is funny.

Based on what I heard from Sister and Auntie, Sister ran away when she was a high school junior and went on a train to Seoul. She immediately ended up in a red light district. After only a few days working as a prostitute, she met Mr. Park while he was on his military leave. After staying overnight without so much as touching her finger, he came back that next afternoon. He yelled at the people in charge and demanded that they let Sister go. They beat up Mr. Park and kicked him out, and Sister

몸이 밑천인데 빚은 무슨 빚?

어느 날 계집애가 하나 찾아왔더구나. 〈김미선이라고
해요. 박일도라는 분 아시죠?〉 화장기 없는 맨얼굴에
티셔츠 걸치고, 대학노트 옆에 끼고 말야. 부아가 안 나
니? 자기가 일도씨 애인인데 일도씨가 나를 잊지 못한
다나? 내가 그랬지. 손 떼라고. 나는 평생 그 남자 못 버
린다고…… 사실 그럴 마음은 조금도 없었어. 샌님이
하도 따라붙어서 그렇지 않아도 어떻게 떼어버리나 궁
리 중이었거든. 그런데 사람 마음이 요상하지, 그 샌님
좋아서 눈물 짜는 여자를 보니까 갑자기 마음이 달라지
는 거 있지? 그러고 몇 달 되었나? 그 여자가 다른 남자
와 결혼한다고 샌님이 전하더구나. 샌님도 마음이 안
좋은가봐, 어깨가 축 처져서 말하는 품이. 그걸 보니 또
화가 치밀더라구. 내가 갔지, 그 여자 결혼식에. 파토 놓
는 기분루다. 꽃다발 하나 들고, 속이 다 들여다뵈는
제일 야한 원피스 입고. 깜짝 놀라지, 물론. 그래도 지금
생각해보면, 미선씨가 보통 여자가 아냐. 침착하더라
구. 나중에 연락하겠다고 전화 번호를 묻는 거야. 글쎄,
나 같으면 흉내도 못 내.

was transferred to another house. Two years later, once again they ran into each other on a street.

"At the time I was working at a hostess bar in Cheongnyangni... He was so formal when he apologized. He said he was sorry that he had gone back to his military service without solving my problems. Wasn't he funny? How could he solve them? I didn't expect anything from him, that gentleman scholar. When I first met him, I was clearly so inexperienced. So, he asked me to just talk overnight. That's why I told him that I'd been abducted and pleaded with him to rescue me. But the truth is, I knew I might end up in a place like that when I ran away from home.

"And then he kept on visiting me at the hostess bar... He was my customer and so I tried to be agreeable to him. What else could I have done? He just kept on saying he was sorry. He even offered me a large sum of money he'd earned working as a tutor, saying that I should use it to pay off my debt to the manageress. Ridiculous! I didn't have any debts from the beginning. I'd bargained with them pretty well. I had my body to sell, so what debts?

"One day, a girl came to see me. 'My name is Kim Mi-seon. You know Pak Il-do, right?' No make-up,

미선씨라는 여자도 주책이다. 전화 통화로 언니에게 남편 흉, 자기 아이 걱정, 별 이야기를 다 늘어놓는다. 언니 역시, 저런, 쯔쯧 힘들겠다 별 맞장구를 다 친다. 미선씨 깐에는 오후 두 시경이면 다방 영업이 한가할 것이라고 그때쯤 하는 모양인데, 공교롭게도 그 시간에는 박 선생님이 다방에 있을 때다. 물론 언니는 미선씨에게 박 선생님이 와 있다는 말은 하지 않는다. 단지 미선씨 이름을 들먹여가며 박 선생님의 표정을 살피곤 하는 것이 고작이다. 박 선생님의 알듯 말듯 한 편안한 미소, 그게 내게는 수수께끼다. 정말 마음이 그렇게 아무렇지 않을 수 있을까? 시한폭탄 같은 언니 성미로 언제 전화에다 박 선생님 얘기를 쏟아놓을지 모르는데 말이다. 대학물을 먹은 인텔리, 그래서 그런가. 아니, 시를 쓰는 사람이라 그런지 모른다.

박 선생님이 시인이라는 말을 언니에게 들었을 때 나는 왜 그동안 그 사실을 눈치채지 못했을까 한심스러웠다. 박 선생님처럼 눈빛이 후들거리는, 눈꺼풀이 얇고 선한 눈초리를 가진 남자를 나는 여태껏 본 적이 없다. 비록 돈벌이 때문에 학원에서 국어를 가르치기는 한다

T-shirt, and a college notebook tucked under her arm. Wouldn't I have gotten upset? She said that she was his girlfriend, and that Il-do could not forget me, huh! So I said, 'Walk away. I can never let him go.'"

"The truth was that I had no intention whatsoever of ever keeping him. In fact, I'd been wondering how I could get rid of this stalking gentleman scholar. But human psychology is a perverse thing. When I saw a woman crying over him, I could feel my heart change, you know? A few months later, that gentleman scholar told me that she was marrying someone else. He seemed dispirited, his shoulders drooping and all. Seeing him like that, I felt myself getting angry all over again."

"So I went to her wedding. I was going to ruin it. I brought a bunch of flowers for her, but I wore my sexiest dress, the kind that's almost transparent. Of course, she was surprised. Still, come to think of it, Mi-seon wasn't a regular chick. She was very calm. She asked me for my phone number, telling me that she was going to call me later. Goodness, I wouldn't have been able to even pretend to be like that."

That woman Mi-seon is senseless. On the phone,

지만, 그가 여느 사람들과 신경구조 자체가 다르다는 것은 나는 벌써부터 짐작하고 있었다. 그리고 그에게는 확실히 남다른 분위기가 있다!

그가 언니를 보기 위해 오는 것은 분명하지만, 언니에게 무엇을 바라는 것은 전혀 없다. 칼국수로 점심을 먹은 후 시집을 읽거나, 무언가를 끄적거리거나, 학생들의 작문을 내놓고 채점을 하거나……. 하루 종일 아무 말 없이 앉아 있다가 그대로 돌아갈 때도 있다. 그럴 때는 박 선생님이 다방 안에 놓인 탁자나 소파 같은, 아무 감각 없는 물건 같은 기분이 드는 게 사실이다. 박 선생님은 항상 창가의 자기 자리에 앉는다. 그리고 창밖을 멍하니 내다보기를 즐긴다. 창밖의 풍경이랬자 승용차두 대가 비비적대며 겨우 빠져나갈 만한 골목과, 일층집에다 앞면만 이층처럼 함석판을 세워 〈새한 이불〉, 〈실로암 안경〉 등의 간판을 단 맞은편의 허수룩한 집들 그리고 그 뒤를 차고앉은 동네 집들이 고작이다. 멀리 하늘가를 따라 나지막히 둘린 흐릿한 산줄기. 그리고 집마당에 군데군데 박혀 있는 감나무, 은행나무…… 그게 전부인 것이다. 박 선생님은 지겹지도 않은지 그

she talks and talks about all kinds of intimate matters. She puts her husband down, worries about her children... Sister also responds with, "My, I'm sorry" and "Oh, no, it must be hard," and so on and so forth. Mi-seon calls Sister around 2 PM, most likely thinking that we wouldn't have many customers around that time. But unfortunately, that's when Mr. Park is in the coffee shop. Of course, Sister doesn't tell Mi-seon that Mr. Park is in the coffee shop. The only thing she does is drop Mi-seon's name, scrutinizing Mr. Park's face while doing so. Mr. Park's mysteriously comfortable smile, that really puzzles me. Is it really possible for him to feel so at ease? Given Sister's ticking time bomb temper, there's no telling when Sister'll start to spout out stories about Mr. Park on the phone. An intellectual, a college graduate—is that how he can stay calm? No, maybe because he's a poet?

When Sister told me that Mr. Park was a poet, I wondered how I could have been so stupid not to notice that already. I've never seen a man like Mr. Park, a man with a trembling glance, thin eyelids, and a good-natured appearance. Although he teaches Korean at a cram school to make money, I've always known that he is constitutionally different

풍경에 몇십 분씩 시선을 박고 있다. 어쩌다 보는 그의 충혈된 눈. 전날 먹은 술이 덜 깬 건지, 아니면 무슨 울적한 심사를 주체하지 못해 얼굴로 비져나오는 건지 간혹 지친 표정을 지을 때가 있을 뿐이다.

언니 역시 박 선생님이 있거나 없거나 그대로 손님을 맞는다. 단골손님에게 아양을 떨고 장난을 걸고…… 박 선생님을 그나마 어려워하는 점이라면 점심을 그와 같이 먹지 않는다는 점이다. 박 선생님에게 따로 주고 그리고 주방 앞 탁자에서 우리 셋이 같이 먹고. 손님으로서의 최소한의 예우는 갖춰주는 셈이다. 하긴 그러니까 칼국수 값을 받을 수 있다. 한 번도 박 선생님에게 점심을 공짜로 대접한 적은 없다. 언니도 참 독한 여자다.

문득 얼굴을 드니 저만치 걸어가던 연인 한 쌍이 가벼운 실랑이를 하고 있다. 남자는 이미 젖은 벤치에 철퍼덕 앉았고 여자는 못 앉겠다고 까탈을 부리는 중이다.

여기 앉으라니까.

남자가 여자에게 자기 무릎을 가리킨다. 한참을 망설이던 여자가 주위를 살피더니—물론 나도 쳐다보고—남자의 무릎에 걸터앉는다. 남자가 우산을 폭 내린다.

from other people, has a different kind of nerve system. And what a unique aura!

He clearly comes to our coffee shop to see Sister, but he does not want anything from her. After eating chopped noodle lunch, he reads a poetry book, scribbles something down, or grades student writing. Sometimes, he just sits still all afternoon and then leaves. In those times, he almost appears to be a prop in the coffee shop, like a table or a sofa, a thing without sensations. Mr. Park always sits in his favorite seat next to the window. He enjoys looking out the window absentmindedly. Outside our shop, the only things to look at is our alleyway that's so narrow two cars can barely cross each other inside of it, the shabby one-story houses with their fake second floor façades made of sheets of zinc, where signs that say "Saehan Comforters" and "Siloam Glasses" hang across the alley, and then, finally our neighborhood houses behind all of this. Much farther in the distance, there's the vague outline of a low mountain range along the edge of the sky. And you can see the persimmon trees and gingko trees here and there sticking out of people's yards. That's all. Mr. Park fixes his glance onto this drab scene for a good

히히덕대는 소리가 간지럽다. 미친 것들. 그러면서도 슬그머니 질투가 난다. 박 선생님은 절대로 내게 자기 무릎에 앉으라고 할 사람이 아니다. 현수라면…… 그리하고도 남는다. 흥, 현수가 아무리 앉으라고 해도 나는 그의 무릎에는 앉지 않는다. 미스 양이라면 냉큼 올라앉겠지. 갑자기 웃음이 난다. 미스 양의 오리 궁둥이라니, 현수 무릎이 저려도 한참 저릴 것이다. 언니는, 언니는 백 사람의 무릎에라도 마다 않고 앉을 여자다. 하여간 언니는 못 말린다. 말도 너무 막 해댄다. 어제 일만 해도 그렇다.

저런 개잡년. 다방 살림 다 들어먹어, 저 쌍년이.

찻잔 하나 깨뜨렸다고 내게 쏟아놓은 욕지거리다. 그깟 낡은 찻잔, 금이 간 지 오래라 다방 손님들도 이것 좀 내버리라고 모두 한마디씩 하던 커피 잔이다.

너무 그러지 말아요, 윤희씨도 이젠 어엿한 숙녀인데.

박 선생님이 말리지만 않았으면 나도 그대로는 안 있었다.

두 사람을 가린 우산이 계속 들먹인다. 괜히 서글픈 생각이 들어서 길가의 벤치로 다가간다. 털썩 주저앉는

long period as if he isn't bored at all. Occasionally, his eyes are red and he looks tired, perhaps because he's hung over, or maybe because his darker thoughts come through from his eyes.

Sister welcomes the other customers warmly whether Mr. Park is there or not. She flirts and plays with the regulars... The only sign that shows that she respects Mr. Park is that she never has lunch with him. After serving him his lunch, the three of us—Sister, Auntie, and me—eat together at a table near the kitchen. It's only in these moments that she treats him respectfully as our customer. Well, that's probably because she charges him for the chopped noodles. She's never treated him with a free lunch. She really is a heartless woman.

I look up and see a couple quarreling mildly. The man has already sat down on a wet bench and the woman refuses to sit.

"Sit here." The man points to his lap. The woman hesitates for a moment, looks around—looks at me, of course—and finally takes a seat on his lap. The man lowers his umbrella abruptly. Their giggles embarrass me. Out of their minds! But, I feel jealous, too. Mr. Park would never ask me to sit on his lap. Maybe, Hyeon-su... He would do that and

다. 스커트가 젖고, 팬티가 젖고…… 궁둥이가 썰렁하게 젖어올수록 가슴도 저릿하게 젖어온다. 새 스커트라고 생각하니, 마치 내가 슬픈 영화의 여주인공 같은 기분이다. 사랑해선 안 될 사람을 사랑하다가 떠나보내고 그와의 추억이 담긴 벤치에 혼자 앉아…… 아, 사랑이란 정말 무엇일까. 내 가슴속을 박 선생님은 정말 모르는 것일까. 그가 이해하려고만 한다면 내 속마음이야 알고도 남을 것이다. 가슴 깊이 저려오는 이 서러움을 이해하지 못한다면 그는 정말 시인도 뭣도 아니다. 나는 우산을 더욱 밑으로 끌어내려 그러잡는다. 이런 때는 눈물을 흘려야 제격인데…… 눈물은 나지 않는다. 언니 같으면 거짓 눈물도 멀쩡히 흘릴 사람이다. 그러나 언니는 박 선생님을 별로 좋아하지 않는다. 언니 말대로, 박 선생님은 언니를 좋아하는 것이 아니라 자기 자신을 사랑하고 있는 것인지도 모른다. 그러고 보면 눈이 찌그러진 주방 아줌마가 더 행복한지도 모른다. 적어도 아줌마는 자기 남자를 자기 방식대로 사랑하며 살고 있으니 말이다.

연인들의 우산이 버쩍 올라가는 듯하더니 그들이 벤

more. Pshaw! I'll never sit on his lap, no matter how much he might beg.

Miss Yang might jump at the opportunity. I suddenly smile to myself. Miss Yang's duck butt, ha! Hyeon-su would be in so much pain with her on his lap. Sister. She wouldn't hesitate to sit on a hundred men's laps. She's something else for sure. What a dirty mouth she's got. That was certainly true yesterday, too.

"You, bitch! You'll destroy everything in this shop. You, stupid bitch!" This is what I got from her just because I broke a single coffee cup. That cup was so old and chipped, even our customers told us to throw it out.

"Please, don't be so harsh with her! Yun-hi is a lady now," Mr. Park said.

But for Mr. Park's sake, I wouldn't have let it go like that, either.

The umbrella hiding the couple continues to bob up and down. I feel sad for no reason. I go to a nearby bench and sit down, my bottom hitting the bench hard. As my skirt, and then my panties get wet, and as my bottom begins to feel wet, I feel my heart begin to grow wet as well. I remember that I'm wearing a new skirt but I feel like a heroine in

치에서 일어선다. 여자의 어깨를 그러안은 남자는 좀 전보다도 어딘가 여자에 대해 자신이 있어 보인다. 그들이 내 앞을 지나면서, 젖은 벤치에 하릴없이 앉아 있는 나를 빤히 쳐다보고 지나간다. 웃음을 억지로 참는 표정이다. 남자의 바지 궁둥이는 색이 진해서 그런지 비에 젖은 표가 잘 나지 않는다. 그리고…… 물론 여자의 바바리 궁둥이는 멀쩡하다. 이게 무슨 꼴이람. 스프링 튕기듯 발딱 일어선다. 새 스커트가 너무 아깝다. 미색의 면 스커트는 남 보기에도 흉칙하게 젖어들었을 것이다. 세상에. 스스로 생각해봐도 나는 정말 대책 없는 년이다. 그렇지만, 후회하지는 말자. 박 선생님의 우산을 다시 바짝 내린다. 시를 쓰는 이의 부인이라면, 이 정도의 희생은 당연한 것이다.

3

홀에 막 들어서는 순간 나는 그만 심장이 멈추는 줄만 알았다. 웬일로 박 선생님이 벌써 와 있는 것이다. 반사적으로 들고 있던 우산을 뒤로 홱 돌린다. 그러고는

some tragic movie. A girl sits alone on a bench rich with her lover's memories, the lover whom she just had to send away because she shouldn't have loved him in the first place...

Ah, what is love, really? Doesn't Mr. Park really know what's in my heart? If he tried, he'd be able to see so easily. If he can't even understand this deep, aching sadness in my heart, he can't be a poet, or anything. I lower my own umbrella, gripping its handle tightly. During moments like these, I suppose I should cry... But I can't cry. Sister would know how to fake crying well. But she doesn't like Mr. Park that much. As she said, Mr. Park might love himself more than he loves her. Come to think of it, Auntie might be happier than Sister. Auntie at least lives, loving the man of her life in the way she wants.

The umbrella hiding the couple has appears higher. The couple gets up from the bench. With his arm around her shoulders, the man looks more confident than before. When they pass by me, they stare at me sitting listlessly on the wet bench. They look as if they can barely manage to hold back their smiles. The bottoms of the guy's pants don't look that wet, probably because they're dark-col-

또 자연스럽지 못한 내 행동에 가슴이 철렁 내려앉는다. 박 선생님이 자기 우산을 알아본 것은 아닐까. 나는 황황히 홀을 건너 내 방으로 들어선다. 빗물이 뚝뚝 긋는 우산을 그대로 방 윗목에 밀어놓는다. 가슴이 쿵쾅거린다. 이래서 사람들이 죄짓고는 못산다고 하는 모양이다.

나는 다른 사람들 물건에 절대로 손대지 않는다. 다른 사람들이 다방에 흘리고 간 돈지갑이라든가 손수건, 하다못해 무어라 적힌 메모쪽지까지 나는 카운터 서랍에 잘 넣어두었다가 돌려주곤 한다. 제 주인을 찾지 못한 장갑, 대학노트, 머리핀, 고장난 만년필 들이 카운터 서랍 하나에 가득이다. 남의 물건에 손대는 것은 정말 나쁜 짓이다. 두칠이 일만 해도 나는 용녀 엄마 편이었다. 칠월 칠석에 낳았다고 이름이 두칠인 그 애는 내 친구 용녀의 동생인데, 마을 점포에서 과자를 훔쳐 먹다가 주인아줌마에게 걸렸다. 용녀 엄마가 장작으로 두칠을 두드려 팼는데 온몸에 멍이 든 것은 물론 손가락을 잘못 얻어맞아 두 개가 부러졌다. 〈아비 없는 후레자식, 손가락 아픈 게 대수냐〉고 병원에도 안 데려가더니 결국

ored. And... of course, the back of the woman's raincoat looks fine. Whoops, what am I doing? I leap up like there's springs in my legs. My new skirt is too precious. My pale yellow cotton skirt must be showing a large wet spot that'll look hideous to everyone else. Goodness! Even I feel that I'm hopeless. Still, I won't regret it. I lower Mr. Park's umbrella again. A poet's wife should consider these kinds of sacrifice natural.

3

The moment I enter the hall, I feel as if my heart has stopped. For whatever reasons, Mr. Park is already there. I swing the umbrella abruptly towards my back. I do this automatically. Then, my heart drops at the thought of how unnatural I must look. Perhaps Mr. Park has already recognized his own umbrella? I rush over to the room across the hall. I shove the umbrella over by the window without shaking off the rain. My heart is pounding. This must be why they say, "It isn't easy to live your life after you commit a crime."

I never steal other people's stuff. I keep things people forget at the coffee house—wallets, hand-

손가락 두 개를 잘라내야 했다. 〈지 새끼를 그래 패다이, 안들 성질 모질다〉고 우리 엄마는 체머리를 흔들었지만, 나는 용녀 엄마가 잘한 일이라 생각한다. 다만 두칠의 손가락이…… 어린아이 손가락은 다시 잘 붙는다고 하는데 얼른 병원에 갈 걸 그랬다고 생각할 뿐이다.

그러나 박 선생님의 우산만큼은 어쩔 수가 없었다. 임자가 누구인지 뻔히 알면서도, 박 선생님의 우산이기 때문에 나는 돌려줄 수 없었다. 그가 앉았던 자리 한쪽 켠에 비스듬히 기대어 놓은 그의 우산을 손에 쥔 순간, 나는 그의 푸근한 손을 마주 잡는 느낌으로 가슴이 꽉 차오른 것이었다. 하는 수 없다. 이렇게 된 이상 얘기가 나오더라도 딱 잡아떼는 수밖에. 〈선생님 우산요? 잃어버리셨어요? 못 봤는데요.〉 나는 눈을 감고 심호흡을 한다.

홀에 다시 나오는데, 박 선생님이 언니와 카운터 앞에 마주 서 있다.

「어디 가긴? 사우나 가지. 맨날 이 시간에 사우나 가는 거, 아직도 몰라요?」

언니가 박 선생님에게 눈을 흘기며 카운터의 철제 현

kerchiefs, even notes with something written on them—in the counter drawer and always return them to their owners. The drawer is full of unclaimed gloves, college notebooks, hairpins, broken fountain pens. It really is a terrible thing to steal someone else's possessions.

I sided with Yong-nyeo's mom about the Du-chil incident. Du-chil is Yong-nyeo's little brother. His name, Du-chil, means two sevens and his parents named him this because he was born on the seventh day of the seventh lunar month. One day, Du-chil was caught red-handed stealing cookies from a village convenience store. His mom punished him by beating him with a piece of firewood. Not only was Du-chil black and blue all over, but also even his fingers were broken. His mother hadn't even taken him to the hospital, though, and had said, "What's the big deal about a little pain in his fingers? He's a single mother's son after all."

In the end, he had to have those two fingers amputated. My mother shook her head and said, "How could she beat her own son so brutally? She's too cruel." But, I think his mom was right to do what she did. My only criticism is that she didn't take Du-chil to the hospital in time. I heard that chil-

금 상자를 쾅 소리나게 닫는다.

「……그럼, 갔다 와요. 그때까지는 있겠지.」

박 선생님이 선 채로 천천히 말하고 손목시계를 들여다본다. 그리고 돌아서서 창가의 자기 자리에 가서 단정히 앉는다. 언니가 그를 쳐다보고 뭔가 말을 하려다가 그만둔다. 다가서는 나를 쳐다본다.

「너는 어딜 그렇게 쏘다니냐? 어머나 미친년, 이 눈탱이 좀 봐. 시퍼래가지고는. 얼른 지우지 못해?」

하여간 내가 밥이다. 아까 당근을 사러 갈 때는 보고도 가만 있더니, 또 생난리를 친다. 박 선생님 앞에서 창피를 주자는 수작인 것이다. 나는 아무 말 하지 않고 카운터 의자에 주저앉는다. 나는 화장도 마음대로 못하나? 자기는 낮도깨비처럼 분을 뒤집어쓰고 머리에 빨간 염색까지 했으면서.

「누구는 좋겠네, 숫처녀 계집애가 죽는다고 따라붙으니.」

박 선생님 쪽으로 고개를 돌려 이죽거리면서, 언니는 비닐로 된 목욕가방을 거머잡고 다방 문을 나선다. 도저히 참을 수 없다. 이건 분명히 주방 아줌마 짓이다! 내

dren's fingers heal very quickly even after they're broken.

But, Mr. Park's umbrella is an exception. Although I knew very well that it was his, I couldn't return it to him, exactly because it was his. The moment I grabbed that umbrella he'd stood a little apart from his seat, I felt moved as if I was holding his hand. I have no other choice. In the situation I am in now, I have to pretend not to know about it. "Your umbrella? Did you lose it? I haven't seen it." I close my eyes and try to take a deep breath.

When I leave for the hall, Mr. Park is face to face with Sister at the counter.

"Where am I going? I'm going to the sauna. You still don't know that I always go to sauna around this time of the day?" Sister says. She scowls at Mr. Park and bangs the cash register drawer shut loudly.

"Okay, then. Do what you have to do. I'll probably be here when you come back," Mr. Park says, still standing in front of the counter, and looking down at his wristwatch. Then, he turns around, goes to his usual seat, and sits down without saying another word. Sister looks at him, about to say something, but then stops. She notices that I'm ap-

가 박 선생님의 스웨터를 짠다고 언니에게 지절지절 고해바친 것이 분명하다.

아줌마는 주방에 있는 둥그런 간이의자에 앉아 한가로이 콩나물을 다듬고 있다. 세상에, 이런 분란을 일으켜놓고 저렇게 뻔뻔하다.

「언니한테 뭐 하러 고자질해요?」

「뭘?」

아줌마가 멀뚱하게 쳐다본다. 찌그러진 눈하고는. 옛말 틀린 것이 하나 없다. 사람이 생긴 대로 논다지 않는가.

「뜨개질 얘기 했죠, 언니한테?」

「할 짓 없으면 자빠져 잠이나 자라, 이년아.」

「도대체 왜 그렇게 간섭이 심해요? 내가 어떻게 살거나.」

「말이야 바른 말이지, 세상에 남자가 없어서 박 선생이냐? 너희 언니는 어쩌라구.」

「말끝마다 언니, 언니. 언니가 뭘요? 언니가 박 선생님 좋아하기나 해요? 발가락의 때만큼도 여기지 않는데.」

proaching her.

"Where have you been? Crazy bitch! Look at those eyelids! So blue! Why don't you go and wipe that off?"

I'm always her easy mark. She saw my eyelids before when I was going out to buy carrots and didn't say anything about it then. And now this! She's trying to embarrass me in front of Mr. Park. Without answering, I sit down on the chair at the counter. Why shouldn't I put on make-up the way I want? She's so powdered on that she looks almost like a ghost. Besides, she's even had her hair dyed red.

"You must be happy! A virgin, desperately in love with you!" Sister cackles, grabs her toiletries and leaves the coffee shop. This must be Auntie's doing! She must have told Sister that I was knitting a sweater for Mr. Park.

Auntie is sitting on a round stool trimming bean sprouts leisurely in the kitchen. Goodness! After raising a storm like this, she can be this shameless!

"Why did you tell Sister?" I immediately demand.

"What did I tell her?"

Auntie stares at me blankly. Look at that crooked eye! Old sayings are always right! Didn't they say

「……이년아, 네가 뭘 아니, 세상 조화 속을.」

아줌마는 갑자기 무슨 민요라도 뽑듯 말에 가락을 붙여 흥얼거린다. 그렇게 세상 조화 속에 달통한 양반이 왜 남편 소박을 당하셔? 한마디 하려다가 입을 다문다. 아줌마가 찌그러진 눈으로 꼬나보면 겁이 나는 것이 사실이다.

오늘의 박 선생님은 바바리코트 차림이다. 잠바나 남방셔츠 따위, 가벼운 옷차림만 보다가 코트를 보니 낯선 사람 같다. 그의 자리 옆에, 못 보던 새 우산이 비스듬히 기대어져 있다. 이번에는 검은색의 체크무늬 우산이다. 손잡이도 전번 것보다 훨씬 짧아 뭉뚱하게 생긴 것이다. 그가 다른 우산을 샀다는 사실이 한편으로 안심이 되면서도 또 한편으로는 맥이 빠진다. 내가 가진 회색 우산에서 그의 손길이 어느새 싹 거둬지는 기분이다. 갑자기 박 선생님이 원망스럽다. 사람이란 옛날 것에 대해서는 쉽사리 잊는 법이다. 그의 머릿속에는 예전의 우산 따위, 잊은 지 오래일 것이다.

창밖을 내다보던 그는 이제 눈을 감았다. 자는 것 같지는 않다. 몸 전체가 딱딱하게 굳어 있다. 무슨 생각을

that a person is, more or less, the sum of their appearance?

"You told her about my knitting, right?"

"If you have nothing better to do, just go to sleep, bitch!"

"Why on earth do you keep interfering with my life? Why do you care?"

"Look, honestly, are there no other men in this world besides Mr. Park? What about your sister?"

"Sister Sister! What about Sister? Does she even like Mr. Park? She doesn't think he's worth the dirt between her toes."

Auntie pauses a little and then says, "Bitch, what do you really know about our lives?"

She says this as if she were humming a merry folk song. I think of snapping back, "So you know so much about life that your husband dumped you, huh?" But I don't. It's true that I feel a little scared of her when I see her scowl at me with that grotesque eye of hers.

Today, Mr. Park is wearing a raincoat. Since I'm used to seeing him in a jumper or a short sleeve shirt, I find it strange. An unfamiliar umbrella is propped obliquely next to his seat. This time, it is a black check. The handle is far shorter and more

저리 골똘히 하는 것일까. 나는 그의 탁자로 가서 소리 나지 않게 얌전히 물컵을 내려놓는다. 다시 카운터로 돌아와 의자에 앉는다. 한눈에 알아볼 수 있을 정도로 그의 얼굴이 초췌하다. 어젯밤 학원 강의가 끝난 후 동료들과 술을 마셨을지도 모른다. 이번엔 또 갑자기 그가 가엾다.

그러니 결혼을 하셔야지요. 내가 해장국을 맛있게 끓여줄 텐데.

사실 나는 해장국을 끓일 줄 모른다. 그러나 언니가 가끔 아줌마에게 부탁해서 몇 번 먹어본 적은 있다. 뭐, 정육점에서 선지피 사오고, 이것저것 야채를 잔뜩 넣고 끓이면 될 것이다.

카세트 라디오에 테이프를 집어넣는다. 〈옛시인의 노래〉가 은은히 흘러나온다. 지난번, 큰길의 24시간 편의점에 가서 내 돈으로 사온 것이다. 박 선생님 이미지와 꼭 맞지 않는가 말이다. 박 선생님을 실제로 보고 노래를 지어도 그렇게 맞출 수는 없을 것이다. 머리카락이 몇 가닥 드리워진 그의 흰 이마에는 굵은 주름이 하나 패었다. 피곤할 때는 휴식이 최고다. 눈을 감은 박 선생

blunt than his previous umbrella. On the one hand I'm relieved to see that he bought a new umbrella. But on the other hand, I'm a little disheartened. It feels as if his hand is no longer on the handle of that gray umbrella. Suddenly, I feel resentful. A human being forgets things so easily. He must have forgotten about his old umbrella for a long time now.

Mr. Park is no longer looking out the window. His eyes are closed now. He doesn't look like he's sleeping, though. His entire body looks tense. What's he thinking about so hard? I go to his table and gently place a glass of water next to him. I go back to the counter and take a seat. At first glance, it is clear that he's had a rough time. He might have drunk with his colleagues at the cram school after his lectures. I suddenly feel sorry for him.

That's why he should marry me. I'd make him a delicious soup to relieve his hangovers.

Actually, I don't know how to make a soup that relieves hangovers. But, I have eaten the soup a few times when Sister asked Auntie to make some for her. It doesn't seem that hard. I'll just have to buy fresh animal blood from a butcher shop and boil it with lots of vegetables.

님이 잠깐이나마 잘 수 있도록, 카세트의 노랫소리를 한껏 줄인다.

다방 문을 수선스레 열고 들어서는 이는 다름 아닌 현수다. 오죽해? 박 선생님은 다방에 들락거려도 어딘가 기품이 있는데, 현수는 들어설 때마다 문에 부딪치든지 아니면 탁자라도 밀어젖히든지 부산스럽기 짝이 없다. 말 한마디라도 조용히 건네는 법이 없다. 자기 깐에는 크게 말하는 것이 남자답다고 생각하는지, 투박진 목소리가 쩡쩡 울린다.

목덜미도 왜 저렇게 굵은지. 사람이 좀 시원스런 맛이 없다. 얼굴이고 어깨고 바라진 품이 바윗돌로 눌러놓은 것 같다. 나는 손발이 억센 남자는 무식해 보여서 싫다. 어깨가 좁고 마른 체격의 남자가 유식해 보인다. 바로 현수와 박 선생님의 차이인 것이다.

기껏해야 운동선수, 가수, 여배우의 스캔들이 화제고, 하는 행동이라고는 TV에 나오는 코미디언 흉내, 아니면 실수하는 척하며 옆에 앉은 여자애들 몸이나 건드리고 낄낄거리는 것이 일인, 풋내 나는 어린애들은 정말 사절이다. 박 선생님을 보라. 그들과는 유가 다르다. 남

I push a cassette tape into a player/radio. "Song of a Poet of Old" trickles out. I bought it at the 24-hour store on the main street with my own money. It goes so well with Mr. Park's image. If you had to make a song based on Mr. Park, you wouldn't be able to come up with a song that would fit him this well. There is a deep wrinkle on his pale forehead over which a few strands of his hair hang. Rest is best when you're tired. I turn the volume down so that Mr. Park can take a nap, now that he's closed his eyes.

Someone bangs the coffee shop door open and enters. Of course, it's none other than Hyeon-su. It's not surprising. Mr. Park is dignified even when he enters or leaves a coffee shop, but Hyeon-su always comes crashing through the door or shoving tables about or something. Just so noisy. He never speaks quietly, either. Perhaps he thinks that speaking loudly is manly. His voice echoes all around the hall.

Also, look at how thick the nape of his neck is! There's nothing refined in him. His face, his shoulders, all of them are thick-set as if they were pressed under a rock. I don't like men with thick hands and feet. They look ignorant. Men with nar-

이 가지지 못한 우수의 그림자가 있지 않은가. 꼬집어 말한다고 흉내낼 수 있는 일이 아니다. 현수 따위에게는 평생 설명해줘도 납득하지 못할, 그야말로 차원이 다른 문제인 것이다.

나는 얼른 카운터에서 일어나 주방으로 향한다. 칼국수 국물이 담긴 큰 솥에서는 아직 김도 오르지 않는다. 나도 모르게 조바심이 난다.

「안녕하세요.」

내 뒤를 따라온 현수가 주방 입구 기둥에 몸을 기우듬하게 버티고 선다.

「왔어?」

아줌마가 현수를 보고 응대한다. 현수가 바지주머니에 손을 찌른 채 나를 보고 빙글빙글 웃는다.

「윤희, 너 오랜만이다? 사람 보구 말 한마디가 없냐?」

넉살은. 골목길에서 만난 지 겨우 한 시간이다, 하기야 아줌마에게 알려서 이될 것은 없다.

「주방까지 쫓아 들어오고 난리야?」

「아이구, 윤희씨, 꿈도 야무지셔. 내가 왜 널 쫓아다니냐? 아줌마 보려고 왔는데. 아줌마, 칼국수 특으루다 한

112

row shoulders and thin bodies look intelligent. That's the very difference between Hyeon-su and Mr. Park. I really don't want to have anything to do with young boys whose only conversation topics are athletes, singers, and scandals involving actresses, whose only actions are imitating comedians or touching girls sitting next to them, feigning accidents, and then giggling. Look at Mr. Park! He's just a different kind of person. Doesn't he have that shadow of melancholy those boys can't even dream of having? No matter how hard you explained it to them, they couldn't imitate that. Even if you explained it to Hyeon-su for an entire lifetime, he wouldn't be able to understand it. They're simply on different levels.

I shoot up from the counter and go to the kitchen. No steam is visible yet from the large cauldron boiling the soup for the chopped noodles. I feel anxious.

"Good morning!" Hyeon-su shows up and leans on the kitchen doorframe.

"Hi!" Auntie says.

Hyeon-su stares and smiles at me, his hands in his pants pockets.

"Hey, Yun-hi, long time no see! You don't say

그릇이요?」

　몸을 홱 돌이켜 주방에서 나오는데 뒤에서 또 한마디.

「치마나 갈아입어라, 물대야를 깔고 앉았나, 푹 젖었
다.」

「아따따, 느이두 처녀총각이라구 연애 거냐? 솜털이
보송보송한 것들이.」

　아줌마가 키득댄다.

「연애가 통곡을 하네. 아줌마, 괜히 참견 말아요!」

　다시 주방으로 돌아가 아줌마에게 일침을 놓는다.

「너네들 씩둑꺅둑하는 게 부럽다. 현수, 얼마나 좋으
냐, 성격 좋지 몸 실하지.」

「아줌마나 실컷 좋아하세요.」

「얘얘 참, 현수야, 윤희가 요새 너 줄려고 쉐타 짠다.」

「그 쉐타가 왜 현수 거예요? 아줌마, 도대체 왜 그래
요?」

　기가 막혀. 현수의 얼굴을 보라. 떡 주기도 전에 김칫
국부터 마신다고 현수 얼굴이 새빨갛다.

「쟤가 뭐, 쉐타나 제대로 짜겠어요?」

　세상에 도둑 배짱이라더니, 말도 안 나온다. 이럴 때

114

hello to the customers?"

The nerve of him! It's been only an hour since we met in the alley. Anyway, Auntie doesn't have to know about all that, I guess.

"Why are you following me to the kitchen? What's with all this fuss?"

"My, Yun-hi, you're really dreaming! Why would I follow you? I came to see Auntie. Auntie, make me some chopped noodles, please. The special ones, you know."

When I whirl back around and try to leave the kitchen, Hyeon-su's voice flies at me from behind. "And change your skirt! Were you sitting over a washbowl? You're soaked!"

"Oh, my! Are you two having a love affair at your age? A little boy and a girl, both of you still with your baby hair?" Auntie giggles.

"Just the words, 'love affair,' hurt my ears! Auntie, don't be ridiculous!" I tell her this when she turns around to go back to her place in the kitchen.

"I envy you two bickering like this. What a good kid Hyeon-su is! So good-natured, and healthy!"

"*You* can like him as much as you want!"

"Hey, Hyeon-su, by the way, Yun-hi is knitting a sweater for you these days."

는 자리를 피하는 게 최고다.

「아줌마, 무슨 헛소리만 해봐요, 가만 안 둬!」

아줌마와 현수가 웃는 소리가 들린다.

카운터 의자에 다시 앉기는 했는데 도대체 아줌마가 신경이 쓰여 죽겠다. 슬그머니 주방 쪽으로 다가가 들어보니 다행히 스웨터 이야기는 아니다. 현수네 할머니가 어떻고 전셋값이 올라서 어떻고 따위다.

현수가 착한 아이라는 건 나도 안다. 식구들끼리도 오순도순 의가 좋은 모양이다. 할머니와 홀어머니, 여동생과 같이 사는데, 팔순이 넘은 할머니도 손자 대학 못 보낸 게 한이라며 시장에서 나물 좌판을 놓고 앉았다한다. 아줌마는 현수가 오면 뭘 못 줘서 안달이다. 아무리 그런들 무엇 하나. 내 마음을 얻기는 틀렸다. 버스는 떠나고 신작로엔 먼지만 풀풀 날리는 것이다!

열한 시 반. 오늘따라 시간이 왜 이렇게 더딘지 알 수없다. 언니도 참 대단한 여자다. 박 선생님이 다른 때보다 한 시간 이상 빨리 나타난 걸 보아도 무슨 중요한 일이 있는 것이 분명한데, 그깟 사우나 하루 빠지면 무슨일이라도 나는가 말이다. 꾹 다물린 박 선생님의 입을

"Wait, you think that sweater his? Auntie, what on earth is wrong with you?"

I'm livid. Look at Hyeon-su's face! "Counting your chickens before they're hatched" could not be more appropriate now. Hyeon-su's face is bright red.

"Does she even know how to knit a sweater?" Hyeon-su says.

Goodness! The nerve of him! I can't even speak. At moments like these, the best solution is just to leave.

"Auntie! If you say any more nonsense, the next time I won't just let it go."

I can hear Auntie and Hyeon-su laugh.

I sit at the counter, but I start to worry again about what Auntie might be saying. I creep back towards the kitchen and listen. Luckily, they're not talking about the sweater, but things like Hyeon-su's grandmother and the rising rent prices.

I know Hyeon-su's a good guy. It seems that his family is all very nice. He lives with his grandmother, single mother, and younger sister. His grandmother of more than eighty years is known to sell vegetables on a sit-down stall in the market, always lamenting that Hyeon-su was never able go

보면 심상찮은 일이 있는 게 분명하다.

이제 생각해보니 언니도 이상하다. 언니 역시, 보통 때 사우나탕에 가는 시간보다 삼십 분 이상 빨리 가버렸다. 언니가 일부러 자리를 피한 것일까.

「이거 미안해서 어쩌지, 윤희씨?」

칼국수 쟁반을 내려놓는 기척에 눈을 뜬 박 선생님은 돌연 손을 내젓는다.

「오늘은 점심을 안 먹으려고. 어디 갈 데가 있어서 말이지.」

「그러세요?」

나는 얼른 쟁반에다 다시 칼국수를 올린다. 하기야 아직 정오도 되지 않았으니 점심때로는 이른 시각이다. 오늘따라 박 선생님이 일찍 와서 서둘러 내갔던 것뿐이다. 주방을 향해 가는데, 탁자에 앉아 칼국수를 입에 가득 문 현수가 박 선생님의 칼국수를 내려놓으라고 젓가락으로 허공을 휘저어댄다. 나는 모른 체하고 그대로 지나친다.

「박 선생님이 안 드신대요.」

「현수나 주렴, 이왕 끓인 거.」

to college. Whenever Hyeon-su comes to our coffee shop, Auntie always wants to give him something. None of this matters to me, though. I'm not
going to be interested in him at all. This bus has
left and there's only dust on the road left for him.

Eleven thirty. I wonder why time goes so slowly
today. Sister is really something else. Judging by
the fact that Mr. Park came more than an hour earlier than usual, there must be something important
going on. So, what's the big deal if she misses going to the sauna once? Mr. Park's sealed mouth also
tells you that clearly something important has come
up.

Come to think of it, Sister is acting strangely, too.
She went to the sauna more than thirty minutes
earlier than usual today. Did she avoid him on purpose?

"I'm so sorry, Yun-hi," Mr. Park says, suddenly
waving his hand. He blinks, his eyes fluttering open
at the sound of my clattering tray.

"I'm not having lunch here today. I have somewhere to go today."

"Oh, yes?"

I hastily put the chopped noodle bowl back on
the tray. It is, in fact, rather early for lunch; it isn't

아줌마가 쟁반을 들여다보며 말을 잇는다. 마침 자리에서 일어나 주방으로 따라 들어온 현수가 아줌마 말을 듣고 금방 희희낙락이다.

「역시 아줌마밖에 없다니까, 내 생각을 해주는 사람은.」

라디오 음악이 조용히 흐른다. 몇 마디 객쩍은 농담을 하던 현수도 제풀에 꺾여 돌아가고 아줌마도 방 안에 들어가버렸는지 인기척이 없다. 오늘따라 박 선생님은 내가 가져다준 신문도 보지 않는다. 바깥 골목도 내다보지 않고 눈을 감았다가, 아니면 탁자 모서리만 뚫어지게 쳐다보며 무언가를 골똘히 생각할 뿐이다. 오로지 그가 하는 행동이라고는 자신의 팔을 들어 손목시계를 본 후, 확인하듯 벽에 걸린 시계에 시선을 주는 것뿐이다.

열두 시 반. 언니는 오지 않는다. 사우나에 간 지 한 시간 반이면 돌아오고도 남았을 시간이다. 오늘따라 무슨 멋을 그렇게 부리는지. 한 시간 반 동안, 나는 두 번 더 박 선생님에게 칼국수를 가져올까요, 물었다. 박 선생님은 그때마다 미소를 지으며 고개를 내저었다. 애꿎은 라디오만 몇 번, 켰다가 껐다. 켜놓자니 수다스런 진

even noon yet. I just brought it to him early because he happened to come by early today. On my way back to the kitchen, Hyeon-su, sitting at a table with his mouth already full of chopped noodles, waves his chopsticks to tell me to leave Mr. Park's chopped noodles at his table. I ignore him and take the tray back to the kitchen.

"Mr. Park isn't having lunch."

"Give it to Hyeon-su. We don't want to waste it," Auntie says, looking at the tray.

Hyeon-su, who has just appeared at the entrance of kitchen, is all smiles at her words.

"Auntie's the only one who's nice to me," Hyeon-su says.

Music trickles out from the radio. After a few un-called-for jokes, Hyeon-su leaves. Auntie also must have left for our room. Unlike other days, Mr. Park isn't reading the newspaper I bring for him. Today, instead of looking out the window he either closes his eyes or stares at the corner of the table in front of him, seemingly deep in thought about something. This afternoon, all he's done is check his watch and then look back at the clock on the wall behind him as if to confirm the time.

Twelve thirty. Sister hasn't come. It's been an

행자의 입담이 그렇고, 끄자니 너무 조용해서 숨도 제대로 쉬지 못할 지경이다. 하여간 언니는 박 선생님의 짝이 아니다. 시인의 아내가 이렇게 무디어서는 안 된다. 언니는 도대체 어디서 무얼 하고 있는 것일까.

이윽고 문이 열리고 언니가 들어선다. 나도 모르게 카운터 의자에서 발딱 일어난다. 사우나에 딸린 미용실에서 화장과 머리손질까지 마친 언니는 오늘따라 무슨 기분 나쁜 일이 있었던 듯 말 한 마디가 없다. 언니는 박 선생님에게 눈길조차 주지 않고 그대로 주방으로 들어간다. 그제서야 나는, 언니 역시 박 선생님 못지않게 긴장해 있음을 깨달았다. 언니가 일부러 늑장을 부린 것이 틀림없는 모양이다.

보리차 컵을 들고 천천히 주방을 나온 언니는 카운터 서랍에서 아스피린을 꺼내어 삼킨다. 그제서야 무슨 결심이라도 한 듯 박 선생님을 똑바로 쳐다본다.

「무슨 일이에요?」

「이삼 일 동안…… 어딜 좀 다녀와야겠소.」

박 선생님이 우산을 들고 자리에서 일어난다. 카운터에 다가선다.

hour and half since she went to the sauna. More than enough time for her to have returned. She must want to look really pretty today. During this hour and half that we've waited for Sister, I asked Mr. Park two more times, "Shall I bring chopped noodles?" Each time, Mr. Park smiles and shakes his head. I turn the innocently piping radio on and off a few times, bothering it for no reason. Turned on, the radio's too noisy, the DJ gabbing and talking his head off. When the radio's off, though, it seems too quiet for me even to breathe. Clearly, Sister is not a good match for Mr. Park. A poet's wife shouldn't be this insensitive. Where on earth is she and what on earth is she doing?

Finally, the door opens and in she comes. Sister, who must have taken care of her hair and make-up at the adjoining beauty salon, does not say a word, as if something unpleasant has happened to her today of all days. Without even so much as a side-long glance at Mr. Park, she marches into the kitchen. I realize, then, that Sister must be as anxious as Mr. Park. She must have been taking this long intentionally.

She comes out from the kitchen, holding a cup of barley tea in her hand. She takes some aspirin pills

「어디요?」

「시골에. 어머니가 편찮으시다는군.」

「학원 강의는 어쩌구?」

「오늘부터 주말까지 나흘 동안 휴가거든. 홀 형수님이 내내 수발하시는데 한번 가봐어야지.」

「그 어머니, 아픈 것도 신식이네. 어떻게 그렇게 자기 휴가 때 딱 맞춰서 아프담?」

「……어머니가 그동안 편찮으신 것, 당신도 알지 않소.」

「글쎄, 그런 거 뭣 땜에 나한테 보고해요? 누가 못 가게 하나?」

언니는 목을 홱 젖히며 쏘아붙인다. 박 선생님은 바바리코트 주머니에 손을 찌른 채 아무 말 없이 그녀를 내려다보고 있다.

「윤희야, 물 한 컵 더 가져와.」

언니는 카운터에 놓은 빈 보리차 컵을 들었다가 쾅 놓는다.

「내일 모레면 올라올거요. 그동안 문단속 잘하고.」

「문단속? 웃겨. 언제 일도씨가 우리 집 문단속 해줬어

from out of the counter drawer and tosses them back. Then, finally, as if she's made up her mind about something, she looks straight at Mr. Park.

"What is it?" she snaps.

"I have to go away... for a few days." Mr. Park says.

Mr. Park picks up his umbrella, gets up, and approaches the counter.

"Where?"

"To my home village. My mother's ill."

"What about your classes?"

"I have a four-day vacation from today to this weekend. My widowed sister-in-law is taking care of my mother. I feel like I should visit them."

"How convenient of your mother, to be ill during your vacation!"

After a short pause, Mr. Park says, "You know that my mother's been ill."

"So, why are you telling this to me? Do you think I'm going to tell you not to go?" Sister snaps her head backwards.

His hands in his coat pockets, Mr. Park looks down at her for a moment.

"Yun-hi, bring me another cup of water!" Sister says, raising her cup and then banging it down on

요? 뭐 하러 올라와? 누가 자기 기다린다구. 자기 엄마 핑계 안 대면 누가 바짓가랑이 잡고 매달릴까봐. 웃겨, 세상. 기도 안 차.」

기관총처럼 퍼붓는 언니의 말을 묵묵히 받아내는 박 선생님. 옆에서 보기에도 민망스럽기 짝이 없다.

「언니.」

보리차를 건네주며 나는 언니의 팔을 꽉 잡는다. 내 마음을 아는지 모르는지 언니는 내 손을 기세 좋게 뿌리친다. 언니는 물 한 컵을 단숨에 들이켠다.

「……갔다 올게.」

박 선생님의 목소리가 차분하다. 언니는 아무 대답이 없다. 어찌된 셈인지 카운터 전화 옆에 놓인 전화요금 통을 뒤집어 몇 개 안 되는 동전을 세기 시작한다. 박 선생님이 이윽고 출입문에 다가서자 신경질적으로 웃으며 악을 쓰기 시작한다.

「잘됐어요. 축하해요. 이제 다시는 여기 안 와도 돼요. 고마워라, 십 년 묵은 체증이 다 뚫리네. 윤희야, 밥 먹자! 배고프다. 아줌마 밥 다 됐수?」

내 가슴이 왜 이렇게 졸아드는지. 언니의 말이 심해서

the counter.

"I'll be back in a few days. Make sure you re-member to lock the doors."

"Lock the doors? You're really funny. When have you cared about my doors? Why are you coming back at all? Who's waiting for you? If you didn't use your mother as an excuse, did you think I wouldn't let you go? You really *are* funny! My God! I'm be-yond speechless."

Mr. Park quietly endures her rapid-fire response, Sister's words coming at him like a hail of bullets. Even I'm embarrassed, just looking at them.

"Sister."

I hand her the cup of barley tea and she tightens the grip on her arm. Whether she knows what I'm thinking or not, she shakes off my hand. She drinks her entire cup of tea without pausing.

After another short pause, Mr. Park replies, his voice serene, "I'll be back."

Sister doesn't answer. Out of the blue, she turns over the bowl of coins next to the telephone on the counter and begins to count the few coins in-side. When Mr. Park finally makes a movement to-wards the coffee shop door, Sister begins to laugh hysterically and calls out:

는 아니었다. 성격이 본래 그런 사람이니 언니에게는
처음부터 기대도 하지 않았다. 박 선생님이 문제였다.
마음 약한 박 선생님이 한순간에 〈그럼, 그만두지 뭐〉
해버릴까봐 내가 마음이 조마조마했던 것이다. 되어먹
지 못한 언니 까탈 때문에, 사내가 자기 어머니에게도
가지 못한대서야 말이 되는가 말이다. 계단을 밟고 내
려가는 박 선생님의 발짝 소리를 듣고서야 나는 겨우
안도의 숨을 쉬었다.

「알게 뭐야? 형수인지 숨겨논 계집인지. 치사한 인간,
누가 자기 붙잡고 매달릴 줄 알구? 아줌마, 밥 먹자니까
뭐 해!」

언니의 앙칼진 목소리. 카운터 앞 소파에 털썩 앉았던
언니는 두 손으로 팔짱을 끼었다가는 이내 풀고 자리에
서 벌떡 일어난다.

「겨우 그 말 하려구 꼭두새벽부터 와서 난리를 쳐? 미
친 자식, 누가 자기 바짓가랑이 붙잡구 늘어질까봐. 속
시원해, 시원하구말구. 사이다 맛이다.」

「윤희 안됐다? 어떡하니, 님이 가버렸으니?」

칼국수 냄비를 내오는 아줌마는 공연히 내게 흰소리

128

"That's wonderful. Congratulations! You don't have to drop by here any more. I'm so grateful. I feel so relieved. Yun-hi! Let's have lunch. I'm hungry. Auntie, is my lunch ready yet?"

I'm so nervous! Not because she's so rude. I don't expect anything less from her given her temper. But I am worried about Mr. Park. Being such a gentle person by nature, I am worried that he might simply say, "I won't go then" after what Sister said. Would it make any sense at all if he didn't visit his mother just because of her nasty temper? Only when I hear his footsteps going down on the stairs do I let out a sigh of relief.

"Who knows? Maybe he's been secretly seeing his sister-in-law or a girl. What a disgrace! Did he expect me to cry and hang onto him? Auntie, what are you doing? I told you to get me lunch."

Her voice is so sharp. Sister, who's sitting heavily on the sofa in front of the counter, unfolds her arms and abruptly stands up.

"Just saying something so stupid to me, he made a such a big deal of it all. Look how early he came even. What a nut! Was he expecting me to hang onto him and beg him not to go? To hang onto his pants when he left? God, I'm relieved. So relieved.

를 늘어놓기 시작한다.

「아줌마는 도대체 아까부터 왜 그래요, 내가 뭘 어쨌다고?」

아무리 내가 아줌마를 째려보아도 아줌마는 내 감정 따위는 안중에도 없다. 오로지 언니 눈치 보기에만 급급하다.

「빌어먹을 인간. 지겨워, 지겨워. 사람팔자를 망쳐놓아두 분수가 있지.」

언니는 다시 소파에 앉으며 주절거린다.

「윤희 너, 현수 괄시하지 마라. 그 사진집 뚱보 계집애하고 붙어다니더라. 요전에도 밤에 둘이서 어디 갔다 오던데?」

아줌마는 혼자 바쁘다. 손으로는 칼국수를 그릇에 덜랴, 찌부러진 눈으로는 내게 계속 눈짓하랴. 언니 비위를 맞춰주라는 신호다.

「됐어요, 현수 같은 애, 두름으로 갖다줘도 안 해요.」

「걔가 어때서? 그만한 녀석도 없구만. 어른 섬길 줄 알지, 착하지, 마음 씀씀이두 넓구.」

그러나 언니에겐 현수 얘기 따위 귀에 들어오지도 않

It's like I just had a drink!"

"Yun-hi, I'm sorry. Your lover left, huh?" Auntie comes in with the pot of noodles and begins her usual talk.

"Auntie, what's the matter with you this morning? Why are you doing this to me?" I protest.

No matter how evil a look I give her, she doesn't care about my feelings one bit. She's too busy trying to read Sister's mind and make herself more agreeable to her.

"Son-of-a-bitch! I'm so tired of him. So tired! He couldn't possibly ruin my life any more!" Sister mutters under her breath, and sits down heavily on the sofa again.

"Yun-hi, don't be so mean to Hyeon-su! I saw him walking around with that fat photo shop girl. Just a few days ago, I saw them coming back from somewhere at night," Auntie raises an eyebrow at me.

Auntie is busy on her own. She puts noodles into the bowls and it looks like she's trying to tell me something with her monster eye. She's trying to tell me that I should be nice to Sister right now.

"I'm fine. I don't want a boy like Hyeon-su, even if I had a dozen of them to choose from."

는 모양이다.

「먹어. 먹어 조겨.」

언니가 젓가락으로 칼국수를 마구 휘젓는다. 그릇에 담긴 국물이 출렁여 쏟아질 듯하다. 아줌마가 언니 앞으로 김치 그릇을 당겨주며 조근조근 말을 잇는다.

「적당히 해둬. 오래 있다가 오는 것도 아니고…… 모레면 온다잖아」

「시원해, 다시는 오지 말았으면 좋겠어. 이럴 때 내가 어디로 영영 없어져버려야 본때를 뵈주는 건데. 칼국수는 웬 허구헌날, 지가 무슨 대통령이라구」

언니는 같은 말을 계속 되뇐다. 이상한 일이다. 수상한 의문이 목까지 꽉 차오른다. 박 선생님이 언니를 짝사랑하는 것이 아니라, 언니도 박 선생님을?…… 그럼 왜 결혼하지 않고 서로 버티는 걸까.

4

오후 세 시가 넘으면서 다방 안은 말 그대로 절간이 되어버렸다. 언니의 호통으로 라디오를 끈 후, 그나마

"What's wrong with him? There aren't many decent boys like him. He respects adults. He's sweet. And he's generous, too."

But, Sister doesn't seem to even hear our chitchat about Hyeon-su.

"Eat! Let's eat up!"

Sister randomly swishes and swirls the noodles. The soup in her bowl looks like it's about to splatter all over the place. Auntie pushes the *kimchi* bowl towards Sister and offers her some advice, "Let it be. He's coming back soon… Didn't he say he'll be back the day after tomorrow?"

"I'm *relieved*. I hope he never comes back. I should teach him a lesson and just disappear forever. Why does he want chopped noodles everyday anyway? Did he really believe that whole president bit?"

She keeps on saying the same thing over and over again. It's very strange. I feel a tight ball in my throat. It's not just Mr. Park who loves her, but she loves him, too? Then, why don't they marry each other? Why fight it?

자리를 잡고 앉았던 대학생 커플이 마저 자리에서 일어
났고—자신들의 목소리가 너무 크게 울리는 게 무척 신
경이 쓰이는 모양이었다—그들이 나가며 들어선 중씰
한 사내 둘은 다방을 휘이 둘러보더니 입에서 내놓은
단 한마디가 〈나가지〉였다. 손님이 하나도 없다면, 그럴
만한 이유가 분명히 있을 것이라는 투였다. 언니의 독
기 서린 신경질을 맞으면서 자리 잡을 손님은 아무도
없을 것이다. 나나 주방 아줌마조차 언니 눈에 안 띄는
구석을 찾아다니는 판이었기 때문이다.

　언니는 잠시도 한자리에 머물러 있지 않는다. 계속 홀
안을 바장이며 투덜거린다. 장사 따위, 안중에도 없는
것 같았다. 주방 아줌마는 하여간 백 년 묵은 여우임에
틀림없다. 주방에 하루 종일 틀어놓는 라디오도 어느새
꺼버렸고, 아예 주방 뒤쪽 베란다로 나가서 며칠 전부
터 별렀던 밑반찬 단지들을 점검하고 있다. 내가 주방
에 들어갈 때마다 베란다에서 얼굴을 들이밀어 언니의
동태를 묻고는, 얼른 언니 옆에 가 있으라고 또 채근을
하는 것이다.

　카운터 앞에 선 언니는 우악스럽게 서랍을 뒤진다. 솔

4

After 3 PM the coffee shop's almost like a Buddhist temple. At Sister's yelping request, I turn off
the radio and then the college student couple who
have been trying to settle down for a while stand
up. They seem bothered by their voice echoing too
loudly in the hall. Two middle-aged men come in
when the young couple leaves, look around, and
utter just one phrase to sum up the state of affairs
at our coffee shop: "Let's go." No customer would
want a table here after witnessing Sister's poison-
ous hysteria. Even Auntie and I are trying to find a
place where we might be invisible to her.

Sister can't sit still. She keeps walking back and
forth, muttering to herself. She looks as if she has
no interest whatsoever in doing business.

Anyway, Auntie must be a hundred-year-old fox.
She's already turned off the radio she usually leaves
on all day. She actually went out to the veranda
behind the kitchen and is now examining the ce-
ramic pots where she keeps pickled side dishes,
something she has been meaning to do for a few
days. Whenever I go to the kitchen, she sticks her
face out from the veranda and asks me how Sister

빗을 찾아 손에 든 언니는 미용실에서 일껏 올린 머리를 마구 빗어내리기 시작한다. 미친년, 이것도 머리라고 해놔? 육천 원이나 받아먹으면서. 괜찮은데요, 뭐. 맨날 그 머리잖아요. 눈이 삐었니? 이게 괜찮게. 멀쩡한 여자를 가지고 할망구를 만들어도 유분수지. 뒤통수에 비녀로 쪽 지을 일 있어? 재수 옴 붙었어. 머리 하나 제대로 만지지 못하면서 뭐러 미용실 간판은 붙여놓는지. 징그러워, 인간들 징그러워.

언니의 표독스런 눈은 슬그머니 자리를 피하려는 내게 꽂힌다. 오나가나 스커트가 말썽이다. 이런 잡년, 암내 풍기느라고 요살을 떠는구나. 밑엣도리를 아예 벗구 다니지 그러니? 허구헌날 바다에 들어가 물질하는 니 에미를 생각해봐라. 괜찮은 사내 하나 물면 팔자 고칠 것 같지? 미친년아, 냉수 먹고 속 차려. 머리꼭지에 피도 안 마른 년이 몸 팔아 무슨 영화를 보겠다구. 그 따위로 몸 굴리면 난 네 꼴 안 본다. 내 손으로 너 목 졸라 죽여버리지. 뭘 빤히 쳐다봐. 그러구두 잘했다는 거야?

언니의 불벼락은 건물 계단에도 떨어진다. 계단에 박은 쇠편자가 들떠서 사람들이 지날 때마다 챙챙거리는

is doing. Then, she urges me to hurry back to Sister.

Sister stands in front of the counter and randomly ransacks a drawer. After finally finding a brush, she randomly combs her hair down, the hair she did up at the beauty salon. "Crazy bitch! How dare she calls this hair? She charged six thousand won for this!" she mutters.

"It looks fine. That's how you always do your hair," I say.

"Something's the matter with your eye? You think this is fine? That bitch turned me into a granny! Why would she give me traditional married woman knot? For me! This is bad karma. Why does she have that "Beauty Salon" sign when she can't even take care of a single hair-do? So disgusting! Everything's so disgusting!"

Her eyes dart to me while I try to slip away. But that skirt of mine is trouble everywhere today. "You, little bitch! Look at how crafty you are, trying to send out your female odor to men! Why don't you just take off all your underwear? Remember your mother who have to spend day and night diving? You think you'll change your fortune, if you meet a decent guy, huh? You, crazy bitch! Have a

데 그 소리가 언니를 자극한 모양이다. 세상의 구두쇠 주인놈. 그 생긴 것 좀 봐라, 맨들맨들한 얼굴에 얌통머리가 없게 생겼잖니. 사람들이 그렇게 오르내리는데 계단 하나 손질해주지 않고. 그러게 라디오를 좀 틀어놓을까요. 이년은 라디오 귀신이 붙었나? 시끄럽게 무슨 라디오야?

다방에서 문을 닫고 있으면 계단의 발짝 소리는 사실 잘 들리지도 않는다. 내 방에서 들리는 빗소리에 비하면 정말 아무것도 아니다. 불같이 화를 내는 중간중간에도 언니가 귀 기울여 계단의 발짝 소리에 신경을 쓰고 있다는 사실은 새로운 발견이었다. 간간이 들리는 발짝 소리가 삼층으로 이어질 때마다 언니의 화가 더욱 돋궈지는 것을 눈치 없는 나는 한참 후에야 알았던 것이다.

마른 걸레에 물을 축여 탁자 위를 꼼꼼히 닦기 시작한다. 아침 청소를 다하기는 했지만, 광택이 죽은 헌 탁자는 물기가 마르기만 하면 금세 구저분해 보인다. 내 기분도 이상스레 착잡하다. 아니, 착잡함을 지나서 참 담하기까지 하다. 언니가 짜증을 내면 낼수록, 교양머리라고는 찾아볼 수 없는 언니의 욕설이 심해지면 심해

cold drink and wake up! What kind of life do you think you can get selling your body? You're still a baby. If you treat your body like that, I'm not going to just leave you alone. I'm gonna strangle you with my own bare hands. What are you staring at? You think you're doing a good job with that outfit?"

Sister spews out poison regarding the building's stairs, too. The stairs make a clanging sound whenever people step on them because of the loosened iron edges. That noise must have provoked her. "That miser landlord! Just look at him. That face fits a shameless person like him. He doesn't take care of the stairs, and so many people go up and down it everyday!"

"So, should I turn on the radio?" I ask.

"Are you haunted by the radio ghost? Radio? What radio? You want noise?"

Actually, if you close the door you can't really hear the footsteps from the stairs. That noise is nothing, compared to the noise from the rain I can hear from our room. I realize that she has been attentively listening to the steps on the stairs even while she's been spitting out all these angry words. Whenever the occasional footsteps disappear towards the third floor, she gets angrier. I am so

질수록, 박 선생님이 내게서 멀어져갔기 때문이다. 내가 알지 못하는 무엇인가가 둘 사이에 있다. 끈. 두 사람을 꽁꽁 묶어놓은 끈. ……서울 생활을 한 것이 작년 9월부터이니 이번 달로 9개월째지만, 사실 나는 언니가 이렇게 불안해하는 것을 처음 보았다. 그제서야 나는 박 선생님이 다방의 정기휴일을 제외하고는 지난 9개월 동안 하루도 빠짐없이 다방에 나왔음을 깨달았다. 사정이 있어서 한두 시간 늦게 나오거나 한 적은 있어도, 그가 고의로 다방에 오지 않은 적이 단 한 번도 없었던 것이다!

물론 내게 이로운 쪽으로 생각할 수도 있다. 언니가 박 선생님을 좋아하는 데 비해, 박 선생님이 언니를 좋아하지 않으니까 언니가 저렇게 화를 낸다거나, 또는 그동안이야 어찌 되었건 오늘 박 선생님이 언니를 본때 있게 무시한 것으로 보아 앞으로 둘 사이는 벌어진다 따위로 말이다. 그러나 내 기분이 왜 이렇게 엉망이 되어가는 것일까. 딴 생각을 하려고 무진 애를 썼는데도 그것조차 되지 않는다. 〈언니가 박 선생님을 좋아한다.〉 그 사실을 내가 너무 쉽게 지나쳐버렸던가. 몇 시간 전

clueless that I realize it this long after it has been going on.

I wet the dry rag and begin to clean tables. I did clean them in the morning as I was supposed to, but those old tables look shabby as soon as they dry because they've lost their luster long ago. I somehow have oddly mixed feelings. No, I don't just have mixed feelings. I feel pretty miserable. The more annoyed Sister gets and the cruder her cursing becomes, the farther Mr. Park goes away from me. There is something between them, something I don't know about. A tie that binds them... I've been in Seoul for nine months since I came here last September. This is the first time I've seen her this anxious. Then, I realize that Mr. Park has come to the coffee shop every single day without exception for the past nine months. He may have been late an hour or two because of some circumstances, but as long as the shop's been open he's never been absent even once!

Of course, I can interpret this whole current situation to my advantage. She's so angry because Mr. Park doesn't like her as much as she likes him. Or, whatever happened in the past, the way Mr. Park ignored Sister so openly today indicates that their

만 해도 나는 언니를 상대로 어떻게든 싸워 이길 준비
가 당당히 되어 있지 않았던가.

박 선생님의 스웨터가 아니라 영배 조끼나 짤 걸 그
랬나 보다. 세상에 남매라고는 단 둘인데, 나는 영배에
게 너무 무심한 누나다. 떨어져 살다보니 더욱 그렇다.
지난 아홉 달 동안 꼭 한번 소포로 학용품 나부랭이를
부쳐주었을 뿐이다. 아침마다 도시락은 제대로 챙겨 가
는지. 중학을 졸업하고 서울에 올라오기 전까지 반 년
남짓한 동안 영배에게 도시락을 챙겨준 일이 그나마 위
안이 된다. 갑자기 엄마도 보고 싶다. 새벽마다 선착장
에 나가 고기를 받아와서 버스 정류장에 좌판을 벌이는
우리 엄마. 아침 아홉 시면 좌판을 거두고 집에 돌아오
는 시간인데, 나는 요새 그 시간엔 꿈나라다. 겉으로는
우락부락하고 드세기 짝이 없는 과부댁이지만 우리 엄
마처럼 속내 고운 이도 드물다.

아지매 잘 위하거래이. 따지고 보면 그 아아도 불쌍한
아아니라.

엄마에게 당숙이 되는 언니의 아버지는 수협에 다니
는 공무원이었다고 했다. 선착장 술집 작부와 눈이 맞

relationship is about to end. Still, why do I feel this miserable? Although I've been trying very hard to turn my attention to something else, I haven't been successful. *Sister likes Mr. Park.* Was I too quick to ignore the signs? Wasn't I so ready to fight off Sister over Mr. Park just a few hours ago?

I should have knitted Yeong-bae's vest instead of Mr. Park's sweater. We're each other's only brother and sister. I've been too indifferent to him. It's been worse because we live so far apart. I sent him just one package of school supplies in the last nine months. I wonder if he takes care to pack his lunch every morning. I feel a little better remembering that I took care of his lunch for about six months after I graduated from middle school until I came to Seoul. Suddenly, I miss Mom. Mom goes to the wharf early every morning to buy fish and sells them at the bus station on a roadside sit-down stall. At 9 AM she gathers her stuff and comes back home. That's when I'm still in the dream world. She looks like a rough-looking widow, but you can rarely find someone as kind-hearted as her.

"Take good care of your aunt. She deserves our sympathy no matter what," Mom said to me.

Mom's uncle and Sister's father was a civil servant

아서는 공금까지 가로채 둘이서 줄행랑을 치고, 몇 달 뒤부터 웬 배 타는 남자가 그 집에 들락거리고…… 어느 날 언니의 엄마가 마을 우물에 빠져 죽었다고 한다. 그 집에 드나들던 사내가 언니의 엄마와 정을 나누면서, 또 한편으로 그때 겨우 여덟 살이었던 언니를 집적였다는 것이다. 엄마가 죽은 후, 언니는 큰아버지 집에 얹혀살았다. 언니네가 살던 집을 큰아버지가 가지기로 하고 그럭저럭 고등학교까지는 다녔는데, 깔끄랑벼 같은 큰어머니의 구박이 또한 말도 못한 모양이었다.

작년, 감포에 놀러왔던 언니를 버스 정류장에 앉은 엄마가 우연히 만나기까지 근 십 년 동안, 엄마는 언니가 서울 어딘가에서 꼭 죽은 줄로만 알았다고 했다. 애처러버 우야노 우리 동생. 불쌍해서 어쩌누 우리 성. 두 사람 사이에 쌓였던 회포는 이틀 밤낮을 두고 울고 웃어도 다 풀리지 않았다.

그저 아지매 하라는 대로만 하거래이. 니한테 절대로 나쁘게는 안 할끼구마는. 아무래도 대처가 안 낫겠나, 시집을 간다 캐도.

서울에 간다고 신이 나서 출싹대는 내게 겨울 내복을

144

who worked at the National Fisheries Cooperative Union. One day he ran away with a barmaid at the wharf, taking the public money he embezzled with him. A few months later, a strange man began visiting her house. Then, one day, Sister's mom threw herself into a village well to her death. That stranger, her mom's lover, also sexually abused Sister. She was only eight years old at the time. After her mother's suicide, she lived with her uncle's family. Her uncle's family sent her to high school in exchange for her family house. But, the abuse from her aunt seemed to have been unbearable. For the ten years until the last year when Mom happened to run into Sister, who happened to be visiting Gampo, Mom had thought she'd died somewhere in Seoul. "My poor, poor little sister!" "My dear, poor big sister!" Two days and two nights, they talked and talked, laughing and crying. It didn't seem enough for them.

"Just listen to your aunt, okay? She won't make you do bad things for you. A big city would be better for you. Especially by the time when you're ready to marry," Mom said to me.

I was so excited to see Seoul. As she packed long johns for me, Mom seemed satisfied that she

챙겨주며, 엄마는 큰 배경을 얻은 듯 흐뭇해했다.

언니가 술을 마시기 시작한 것은 네 시가 조금 넘어서부터다. 밤에 오는 단골들 몫으로 준비해놓는 국산양주를 가져와 혼자 홀짝이기 시작한 것이다.

펌프회사 사장을 놓지 말았어야 했는데. 그 너구리가 그래도 사람은 괜찮았어. 딸만 둘이라며, 나보고 아들하나 낳자고 덤비데. 어느 날 마누라라는 게 쳐들어왔는데, 머리끄덩이 쥐는 품이 벌써 상습이야. 멀쩡한 아들이 둘이나 있다나. 나라구 뭐 녹녹한가? 배에 들지도 않은 애 지우는 조건으루 목돈 좀 울궈냈지. 그 돈이 이 다방 보증금이 되었지만. ……치사하다야. 내가 지금껏 사내들 바짓가랑이 잡아본 적이 없다. 샌님도 그래, 내가 언제 자기보고 뭐라고 했나? 대학교를 졸업하고 어느 회사에 취직이 되어 한두 달 다니더니 어느 날 직장을 그만두었다는 거야. 월급이 너무 작아서 안 되겠다나. 학원의 국어 선생으로 나간다구 그러더라. 시골에 있는 어머니에게 생활비를 부쳐주더라구, 조카들 학비도 대야 한다고 하고. 거머리 같은 인간. 잘됐어, 잘됐어. 벌써 떠났어야지. 결혼해서 자식 낳구 살아야지 뭣

had Sister to look after me in Seoul.

Sister began drinking a little past 4 PM. She brought the domestic whiskey that we prepared for our regulars at night and began drinking it little by little.

"I shouldn't have let go of that pump company president. That raccoon was not a bad guy after all. He said he only had two daughters but he proposed that we have a son together. One day, a woman claiming he was his wife showed up. Judging by the way she went at my hair, she was a veteran at dealing with her husband's mistresses. It turned out that he had two sons. So, was I going to let it all go that easy? I extorted them for a lump sum by pretending that I was pregnant and that I needed an abortion. That money became the seed money for this coffee shop.

"Disgraceful! I've never hung onto guys so far. Speaking of that gentleman scholar, do you think I would have asked anything from him? After graduating from college, he got a job at a company. But, then, after only two months, he quit his job, saying that the salary was too low. He said, instead he'd gotten a job at a cram school, teaching Korean. He supports his mother in the countryside, and helps

147

땜에 내 뒤는 따라다녀.

조그만 양주잔으로 성이 안 차는지 병나발을 불기 시작하는 것을 보고 나는 언니에게 다가섰다.

「좀 천천히 마셔요.」

「여기 좀 앉아봐라, 말 좀 하자. 그래, 네년은 그 샌님 어디가 그리 좋더냐?」

「아 아녜요, 난.」

「뭘 그래? 내가 중간에서 다리를 놓아줄 수도 있어. 내가 그 샌님하고 몸을 섞은 적이 있나. ……사실 그 사람이라면 처자식 고생은 안 시킬 거다. 너야 시집 못 갈 이유도 없지. 나처럼 사내를 받긴 했냐, 꿀릴 게 뭐 있냐.」

언니의 핏발선 눈이 내 눈 속을 꿰뚫는다. 겁이 더럭 난다. 위아래 눈꺼풀에 과장되게 그린 눈화장 때문만은 아니다. 무엇이든 활활 불에 태워버릴 것 같은 눈초리. 언니에게 없는 〈순결〉이라는 것이 여자들의 몸에 지니고 있는 문서라면 온 세상의 여자들을 그대로 불태워 죽여버릴 것 같은, 원망에 가득 찬 눈초리였다. 나도 모르게 말이 더듬거려졌다.

his nephews with their tuitions. He was just cling-
ing to me—like a leech! It's all good now anyway!
He should have left already. He should have married and had children already. Why hold onto me?"

Dissatisfied with her small glass of liquor, Sister
begins to drink straight from the bottle.

I go to her and say, "Please drink slowly."

"Sit here. Let's have a little talk. So, why do you
like that gentleman scholar? What do you like so
much about him?"

"No, no. I..."

"Don't be shy! I can be the matchmaker. I haven't
slept with him, you know." After a pause she continues, "Actually, he is the kind of a guy who
wouldn't make his family suffer. You have no reason not to marry him. You haven't slept with anyone. You have nothing to be ashamed of."

Sister's bloodshot eyes pierce mine. I get really
scared. It's not because of her exaggerated eye
make-up, the dark lines both above and below her
eyes. It's her eyes that seem about to burn. If vir-
ginity were a sort of document that women carried
with them on their bodies, Sister wouldn't hesitate
to burn every woman in the world with her eyes.
Her eyes seemed full of this kind of resentment.

「아녜요, 나 난. 난 그저 형부처럼, 아니 아저씨처럼 그렇게 따랐을 뿐이지. 박 선생님한테도 언니밖에 없잖아요?」

말을 억지로 뱉고 나니 확실히 그런 것 같다. 내가 박 선생님을 따른 감정이야 사랑이라고 말할 수는 없을 것이다. 그리고 말이야 바른 말이지, 박 선생님한테 나 같은 아이 안중에나 있었나. 나이도 두 배 가까운데. 내게서 시선을 거둔 언니는 한참 눈을 감고 있다.

「시골 얘기 좀 하데?」

「예, 바닷가라니까 언제 한번 가보고 싶다고.」

「누가 느이 시골 얘기야? 그 인간 시골에 있는 식구 얘기하더냐니깐?」

「형수가 어머니 모시고 사신다잖아요? 어머니가 편찮으셔서.」

「미친년, 그걸 믿냐? 형수는 무슨 놈의 형수? 형수가 왜 혼자 살아? 제 마누라지. 사내 말을 믿냐? 아줌마, 여기 술 한 병 더 가져와요.」

언니가 버럭 소리를 지르는 통에 나는 깜짝 놀라 자리에서 일어나고 말았다. 술 한 병은 이미 바닥이 났다.

I stammer without knowing it, "No. I—I—I just like him. As if he was my brother-in-law. He only loves you, though, doesn't he?"

Blurting all this out, I feel as if that was what I've been feeling all along. You can't call my feelings towards him love. Also, truth be told, has he even been aware of my presence? He's almost twice as old as me. Sister seems about to say something but then pauses. She closes her eyes and her eyes stay closed for a long time.

"Did he talk about the countryside?" Sister asks.

"Yes. I told him I'm from a seaside village. He said he wanted to visit some time."

"Who was asking about your countryside? Has he ever told you anything about *his* family in the countryside?"

"Didn't he say that his sister-in-law is taking care of his mother there? Because his mother's sick?"

"You—you dumb bitch! Do you really believe that? What sister-in-law? Why would his sister-in-law live alone with his mother? It's his wife. Do you really believe everything that men say? Auntie, please bring me another bottle!"

Her sudden outburst surprises me and I stand up. Her bottle is empty. Sister sways back and forth

얼굴이 벌건 채로 윗몸을 끄덕이는 언니는 이미 평상시의 언니가 아니다. 주방에서 나온 아줌마는 빈손이다. 나무라듯 언니를 타이른다.

「뭘 그렇게 신경 써? 낼모레면 온다는데. 그 샌님이 안 오구 배겨? 자기가 누구야? 그렇게 자신이 없어?」

「아줌마가 뭘 알아? 그 인간 속을. 형수는 무슨 형수.」

「자기 엄마가 아프다는데 가봐야지 어떡해? 욕심두 사납지, 어떻게 그리 꼼짝 않구 자기만 쳐다보라구 그래?」

「내가 언제? 아줌마 사람 잡네. 정말야, 시원하다니까. 그 인간 다시는 얼씬도 말아야 할 텐데. 와서 뭐 좋은 일 있다구. 나는 벌써부터 끝이었어. 내가 뭐래? 난 싫어. 지겨워, 그 인간.」

아줌마가 기가 막히다는 듯 피식 웃는다.

「아이구, 말은 그렇게 떵떵거려도 내 다 아네. 칼국수만 해도 그래. 맨날 끓이는 이유가 그 사람 주려는 것 아니야? 자기는 가루 음식 즐기지도 않으면서.」

「내…… 인간이 불쌍해서…… 허구헌날 우리 집에 와서 사니까 그냥 잘 먹는 거 해주자는 거였지, 뭐 내

and her face is completely flushed. She's not at all like her usual self. Auntie comes out from the kitchen, but without a liquor bottle. She tries to calm Sister down, gently reproving her.

"Why all this fuss? Didn't he say that he's coming back in a day or two? Can that gentleman scholar even stand not visiting you? You're you! Are you so unsure of yourself?"

"What do you know about what he's really up to? Sister-in-law my ass!"

"Didn't he say his mother was ill? Does he have any choice except to visit his mother? Stop being so greedy! How could you expect him to only look at you every day?"

"What are you talking about? When did I say anything like that? You're accusing me unjustly. I mean it! I'm relieved! I hope he never comes back. What good does he do coming here anyway? It's been over with him for a long time. What did I tell you? I don't like him. I'm sick and tired of him."

Auntie grins, clearly not buying a word of what Sister says.

"Oh, yes! No matter what you say, I know what your true feelings are. Just look at these chopped noodles. Why do we make them every day except

가…… 잘됐어, 잘됐어. 시골 내려가서 아예 다시는 서울바닥에 나타나지도 마라고 그래. 홀어머니 좋아하네, 괜히 핑계 댈 것 없으니까?」

「글쎄, 걱정 말라니까! 와요 와.」

아줌마가 버럭 화를 낸다. 언니가 또 갑자기 나를 쏘아본다.

「미친년. 머리에 피도 안 마른 게 눈탱이는 시퍼래가지구. 내일 아침 차루 당장 시골 내려가라. 느이 에미 밑에 있다가 웬만한 자리 있으면 시집 가. 이런 데 있다가 몸 버리고 신세 망치는 거 빤한 거 아니냐구. ……아줌마도 떠나, 떠나라구! 이놈의 장사 지긋지긋해. 돈 벌어 건물세 내기 바쁘구. 아줌마야 어디 간들 그 월급 못 받겠어? 다 때려치워야지. 이꼴 저꼴 안 보려면.」

아줌마가 말 한마디 없이 주방으로 들어간다. 주방을 슬쩍 들여다보니, 아줌마는 한가로이 물걸레로 주방 벽을 닦고 있다.

소파에 기댄 언니는 앉은 채로 잠이 들었다. 카운터 의자에 다시 앉은 나는 머리에 물이라도 끼얹은 듯 더욱 정신이 맑아진다. 어떤 일에서건 자신만만하고 당차

for him? You don't even like wheat!"

"I... took pity on him... He practically lives here and I just wanted to feed him what he likes. That's all... Well, it's better this way. It's really better. Let him go to the countryside and never come back to Seoul. A single mother? Could he come up with a worse excuse?"

"Oh my—don't worry about it! He's coming back. I know it!" Auntie practically yells at Sister.

Sister suddenly glares at me.

"Crazy bitch! A baby like you wearing blue eye shadow! Why don't you go back home tomorrow! Go live with your mom and find a decent man to marry! Hang out around a place like this too long and it's already decided that you'll ruin your body and your life!" Sister pauses for a moment, and then continues impulsively: "Auntie, you, get out of here, too! Please! I'm sick and tired of this business. I make money just to pay rent, that's all. Wherever you go, wouldn't you make as much somewhere as you'd make here? God, I should just quit! I don't want to be bothered any more!"

Auntie doesn't respond and returns to the kitchen. I take a peek into the kitchen. Auntie is wiping the kitchen walls with a wet rag as if nothing's the

던 언니는 이제 없다. 제 신세타령에 지친 술 취한 작부가 소파에 늘어져 있을 뿐이다. 아줌마의 찌그러진 눈, 언니의 축 늘어진 몸뚱이. 네가 뭘 아니, 세상 조화 속을. 아줌마의 홍얼대던 말소리가 다시 들리는 것 같다.

최사장은 저녁 일곱 시가 조금 안 되어서 왔다. 사람 마음이 참 요상하다. 언제 봐도 술 취한 사람처럼 불콰한 얼굴에 벽장코, 사나흘에 한 번씩 저녁에 와서 술잔을 기울이는 최사장이 사기꾼 같아서 나는 항상 달갑지 않았는데, 오늘따라 무척 반갑다. 최사장이라면 언니 기분을 바꿔줄 수도 있으리라는 기대 때문이다. 골목 바깥 큰길에서 부동산 사무실을 가지고 있는 그는 부품하게 웃기는 소리를 잘한다.

「오셨어요?」

반가이 맞는 나를 보고, 최사장은 새삼스런 표정으로 내 몸을 훑는다.

「야, 우리 애기, 이제 보니 한창 물이 올랐구나. 허리도 한들한들 꺾어지는 게.」

보리차 잔을 가져다가 얼른 언니가 앉은 탁자에 놓는다. 소파에 퍼드러져 앉아 알은 체도 않는 언니를 최사

matter.

Sister is now suddenly asleep, leaning up against the sofa. I take a seat down on the counter chair again; I feel clear-headed, as if I'd just taken a cold shower. There's no longer the brave and confident Sister. Just a drunken prostitute, exhausted after her tale of woe, prostrate. Auntie's grotesque eye, Sister's prostrate body. I seem to hear Auntie humming again, "what do you really know about our lives?"

President Choe enters a little before seven. A human heart is a strange thing. I've never been very glad to see him, this man with his bright red face and pug nose, who comes every three or four days in the evening to drink.

But today, I'm overjoyed to see him. I'm hoping he can change Sister's mood. The president of a real estate agency with an office on the main street is good at jokes.

"Hello, sir!"

Probably surprised to see me welcome him, he runs his eyes across my body.

"Hey, baby, you're blooming! Look at that waist!"

I bring him a cup of barley tea and quickly place it on the table where Sister is sitting. President

장이 손으로 툭 친다.

「어디 아파? 사람이 왔는데 알은 체도 안 하고. 서방
님 오셨구려, 반색을 해야지. 이, 이거 왜 똥 밟은 얼굴
이야, 새서방한테 바람 맞았나.」

「새서방 좋아하네. 마음 통할 서방이나 있으면. 나 같
은 거야 아무려면 어때? 끽해 봤자 물장수년인걸.」

「야야, 기다려라. 한 건만 크게 하면 내, 네 머리 제대
로 올려준다니까.」

최사장이 언니의 허리를 낚아채며 너스레를 떤다. 언
니가 무표정한 얼굴로 최사장 품에 안긴다. 갑자기 언
니가 안되었다는 생각이 든다. 열흘 가는 꽃이 없다는
데, 믿고 살 사내도 자식도 없이 속절없이 늙어만 가면
여자는 참으로 한심할 것이다.

스웨터는 그까짓, 영배 주면 그만이다. 등판을 넓게
짜기 시작했으니, 현수가 달라면 뭐, 현수를 줘도 괜찮
다. 세상에, 나도 어쩌면 이럴 수가 있을까. 박 선생님을
사랑한 것은 아닌 모양이다. 진짜로 사랑했다면 이렇게
간단히 포기할 수는 없을 것이다. 그러면 언니가 박 선
생님에게 느끼는 감정이 사랑일까. 아니면 박 선생님이

Choe taps Sister, prostrate on the sofa and not even pretending to greet him back.

"Hey, are you sick? Whoa, what's wrong with your face? You look like you just stepped on pile of shit. Did your groom stand you up?"

"Groom my ass!" Sister is suddenly awake, "If only I had a loving husband! Who cares about me? I just sell drinks."

"Hey, just wait! If I hit the jackpot, I'll make you my real wife."

President Choe grabs Sister by her waist and begins to jabber away. Expressionless, Sister leaves him alone. Suddenly, I feel sorry for her. They say that no flower lasts for more than ten days. A woman growing old without a husband or children to depend on must feel really wretched.

About that sweater, I guess I can just give it to Yeong-bae. Since I began with just that large back panel, I guess, if Hyeon-su wants it, I can give it to him, too. My goodness! How could I be this way? I guess I really didn't love Mr. Park. If I really loved him, I wouldn't be able to give him up this quickly. If so, then, are Sister's feelings for Mr. Park love? Or, Mr. Park's feelings for Sister? A poor tie. But a strong tie that no one has the right to sever. Is it

언니에게 품는 것이? 잘못 이어진 끈. 그러나 아무도 잘라버릴 권한이 없는 탄탄한 끈. 언니가 박 선생님을 받아들일 수 없는 이유는, 결국 자신이 술집여자 출신이라는 열등감 때문일까. 그래서 내게도 사사건건 간섭했던 것일까.

홀에는 언니와 최사장이 계속 들까불고 있다. 언니의 허리를 끼고 가슴을 만지는 최사장은 오늘따라 장난이 지나친 것 같기도 하다.

창가에 옮겨 앉아 바깥 경치를 바라본다. 빗줄기는 아침보다 한참 약해졌지만 완전히 그치지는 않았다. 어둠이 가득한 골목 바닥에는 우리 다방의 네온사인 불빛이 얼비쳐 울긋불긋하다. 빗물이 번들대는 아스팔트에 번진 색깔들은 어찌 보면 쏟아진 수채화 물감 같기도 하고, 또 어찌 보면 눈물로 얼굴 화장이 엉망이 된 언니 얼굴 같기도 하다. 물론 언니는 울지 않는다. 나는 언니의 눈물을 이제껏 한 번도 본 적이 없다. 속눈썹을 검게 칠한 언니가 울면 검은 눈물이 흐를 것이다.

「이거 얻다 대구 막말을 해, 보자보자하니까?」

무슨 말이 오갔는지 최사장의 목소리에 제법 노기가

because Sister can't overcome her inferiority complex about her prostitute past that she can't accept Mr. Park? Is that why she can't leave me alone about every single little thing I do?

In the hall, Sister and President Choe are rambling and giggling. President Choe seems like he's going too far. He touches Sister's breasts with one hand, while holding her by the waist with the other.

I sit by the window and look out. The rain is lighter than it was in the morning, but it's still raining. The darkened alley road shines with all sorts of colors, reflecting our coffee shop's neon sign. The colors spread on the asphalt and look like a pool of watercolors, or Sister's face with the make-up running and slick with tears. Of course, Sister never cries. I've never seen her cry. With her dark eye make-up on, she'd cry black tears if she did.

"Hey, how dare you talk rudely like that to me? You think I'm just some sleaze?" I can hear President Choe yell. President Choe now sounds pretty angry, although I don't know what made him so angry.

"Oh, no, you're angry! You're much manlier and sexier when you're angry!"

있다.

「화 나셨나봐. 최사장님은 화났을 때가 훨씬 남자답고 섹시하더라.」

언니가 가성으로 깔깔대기 시작한다. 최사장이 하는 수 없이 잠잠해진다. 아무래도 언니의 목소리는 여느 때 같지 않다. 속으로는 검은 눈물을 한참 흩뿌리고 있는지도 모른다. 언니 말대로 박 선생님은 영영 떠나간 것일까. 언니가 처음부터 박 선생님을 만나지 않았더라면 언니는 지금쯤 어떻게 되었을까.

일이 터진 것은 순식간이었다. 뭔가 깨지는 소리가 들리고 어억! 하는 최사장의 비명이 들렸다. 깜짝 놀라 뛰어갔을 때에는 탁자 위에 양주잔이 깨어져 있고 최사장이 왼쪽 눈을 두 손으로 움켜잡고 있었다. 최사장의 뺨으로 피가 흘러내리는 중이었다.

「이년이, 죽고 싶어 환장했나? 이런 벌어먹을 년!」

피가 묻어나는 자신의 손을 보자 최사장이 구둣발로 언니를 지르기 시작한다. 나도 모르게 아줌마를 불러댄다. 주방 아줌마가 잽싸게 뛰어나오더니 소파에 쓰러진 언니를 몸으로 덮친다. 아줌마의 허리에까지 구둣발질

Sister begins to giggle in a loud falsetto. President Choe calms down reluctantly. Sister's voice sounds different, though. Maybe she's shedding black tears in her heart. Did Mr. Park really leave forever like she thinks? What would have happened to her if she never met Mr. Park?

It happens so quickly. Something breaks and President Choe shrieks. I rush over to them. There's a broken liquor bottle on the table, and President Choe is grabbing his left eye with both of his hands. There's a streak of blood flowing down on his cheek.

"Bitch! Are you crazy? You wanna die? You—you son-of-a-bitch!" President Choe suddenly realizes that he's bleeding and sends a leathered shoe foot straight into Sister's midsection. I scream, "Auntie," without knowing that I'm doing it.

Auntie rushes out of the kitchen and covers Sister's body with her own. After kicking Auntie a few times, President Choe reluctantly stops. Luckily, his eyes are fine. Looking at him carefully, I realize that he's not bleeding from his eyes, but from his temple. In the confusion of the moment, I pick up a wet rag and hand it to him. He doesn't even look at it, goes to the counter, picks up a tissue paper, and

을 하던 최사장이 가까스로 동작을 멈춘다. 다행히 눈은 안 다친 모양이다. 자세히 살펴보니 피가 나는 곳은 눈이 아니라 관자놀이다. 나는 엉겁결에 젖은 행주를 가져다 내민다. 최사장은 거들떠보지도 않고 카운터로 다가가 휴지를 상처에 대고 누른다.

「재수 없는 년. 계집이 술주정을 해도 유분수지. 에잇, 술집 것들 곤조라니.」

뒤도 안 돌아보고 문을 나서는 최사장의 뒤통수에 대고, 언니는 아줌마에게 안긴 채로 소리를 지른다.

「티켓 장사? 미친 새끼, 엇다 대고 후림대수작이야? 내가 순진한 계집년들 몸 팔아 돈 챙길 줄 알았니? 세상 말종, 그 돈을 자기가 알겨먹으려구. 저런 새끼는 죽여 버려야 돼. 종로 바닥에 형틀을 매구 목을 매달아 죽여야 돼.」

언니를 겨우 똑바로 앉힌 아줌마가 멍하니 서 있는 나를 툭 친다.

「뭐 해? 얼른 치우지 않고.」

나는 허겁지겁 유리조각을 재떨이에 담기 시작한다.

박 선생님이 제발 돌아와야 할 텐데. 그가 와주지 않

presses it to the wound on his face.

"Bad luck bitch! A girl loses control of herself like this drinking! Fuck! The guts of a barmaid, huh!" President Choe curses a few more times and then leaves.

Still in Auntie's arms, Sister yells after him, "Sell tickets? You crazy asshole! How dare you try to talk me into making money off of innocent girls' bodies? The lowest of the low! And you want a share in it, too, huh? We should execute crooks like you in public! Set up a scaffold in the middle of Jongno Street and hang you right there!"

Auntie sits her up straight and taps me lightly as I stare blankly at the scene in front of me.

"What are you doing? Why don't you start clean-ing up?" she says.

I rush to collect the glass pieces into an ashtray on a table.

I hope Mr. Park comes back. If he doesn't, I wonder what'll happen to Sister. I'm really worried. She used to be so confident and brave when he was around. Why is she acting this pathetic and sad now? I can't stand it. I should have asked Mr. Park where his home village was. I'm so stupid. I don't even know which cram school he teaches at.

으면 언니는 정말 큰일이다. 박 선생님이 있을 때는 매사에 자신만만하고 당차던 언니가, 왜 이렇게 초라하고 불쌍해지는지 정말 못 봐주겠다. 박 선생님 고향이 어디인지 물어봐 두기나 할 걸, 바보 같은 나는 박 선생님이 나가던 입시학원 이름도 모른다.

5

문 잠그지 말어, 잠그면 안 돼.

소파에 쓰러진 채 잠든 언니가 잠꼬대처럼 계속 되뇌던 말은 다방 문에 설치되어 있는 금속 자바라를 채우지 말라는 소리다.

오늘 장사는 글렀는데 문 잠그고 아예 쉬자구.

주방 아줌마의 권유에도 불구하고, 언니는 무슨 생각에선지 문을 열어놓으라는 소리만 되풀이했던 것이다.

머츰하던 비는 다시 굵어졌다. 건물 뒤편에 앉은 털보 아저씨네 지붕 위로 떨어지는 빗소리가 홀에서도 꽤 뚜렷하게 둥당거린다. 아침에 꾸었던 꿈이 다시 생각난다. 박 선생님이 치던 북소리. 꿈땜을 하는 걸 보니, 이

5

"Don't lock the door. Don't, okay?"

That's what Sister, sleeping prostrate on the sofa, keeps muttering as if she's sleep-talking. It means we shouldn't lock the steel lattice shutter outside the coffee shop door.

"It looks like we're done for the day. Let's just lock up and go to bed," Auntie says.

Nevertheless, Sister keeps on insisting that we should leave the door open for what reasons I don't know.

The rain begins to fall harder. The clanging sound from the roof of the hairy uncle's house behind our building is pretty clear in our hall. I'm reminded of my dream this morning. The sound of the drum Mr. Park was beating. The whole event today must have been my way of escaping bad luck by making a lesser sacrifice to offset my bad dream. I must be becoming an adult.

"My dreams were pretty bad. Believe it or not, they always predict what'll happen today!" Mom would sometimes say this in the early morning and then, incredibly, some accident would always befall our village in a day or two. An unexpected storm

제 나도 어른이 되어가나 보다.

꿈자리가 영 편치 않더라이 카네. 내 꿈이 희한하게 맞는데이.

새벽에 엄마가 구시렁거리면 정말 그날이나 이튿날, 마을에 꼭 무슨 일이 있곤 했다. 고깃배가 때 아닌 풍랑을 만나 마을사람들이 마음을 졸인다거나, 아니면 외지로 떠나간 마을사람들의 자식들 중에라도 좋지 않은 일이 있다고 연락이 오는 것이다. 무슨 일 없느냐고 집요하게 마을을 돌아치는 엄마 행동이, 마을사람들을 진짜 걱정해서라기보다는 도리어 그런 일이 터지기를 바라는 엄마의 이상한 심술 같아서 끔찍한 적도 있었다.

박 선생님이 용을 써가며 북을 치는데, 점점 좁혀 들어가던 사람들은 무엇을 뜻하는 것일까. 그리고 그를 향해 손나팔을 만들어 소리 지르던 나는, 도대체 어디에 있었을까. 사람들 틈에도 있지 않고, 새처럼, 먼지처럼 허공에 둥둥 떠다니고 있었을까.

잔주름이 잡힌 언니의 지친 얼굴은 자세히 보니 참 여리게 생겼다. 박 선생님이 자기를 쫓아다니던 이야기를 의기양양하게 늘어놓던 그 자신감은 어디에서도 찾

would worry the villagers, or a bad news about some of children away in large cities would come to the village. Sometimes, when Mom would keep asking other villagers if they'd heard any bad news, I'd shudder at the suspicion that Mom did that not because she was worried about them, but because she wanted something bad to happen to them, and not herself.

What did it mean when the people approached Mr. Park step by step as he beat his drum? And me? Where was I when I was calling him with my hands shaped into a megaphone? I wasn't in the crowd. So, was I floating like a bird, or like a grain of dust?

Upon closer examination, Sister's tired, finely wrinkled face looks very delicate. I can't find any confidence in her face, the confidence that she showed when she was bragging about Mr. Park following her around.

"I asked that gentleman scholar, 'So, if you never forgot about me since we parted ways, when did you go out with Mi-seon?' He was so embarrassed that he didn't know what to say. He said, 'That's Mi-seon's story, and I didn't think we were that way.' So stupid! So, he was basically maintaining that he

아볼 수가 없다.

내가 따졌지, 샘님한테. 〈처음에 나랑 헤어지고 난 후, 한시도 나를 못 잊었다면서 미선씨는 언제 사귀었느냐〉구. 당황해서 어쩔 줄 모르는 거 있지. 〈그건 미선씨 일방적인 생각이고 나는 그렇지 않았다〉나. 숙맥. 술집에서 수십 남자를 거치고 산 내 앞에서 자기는 깨끗하다고 주장하는 건 또 뭐냐. 재수 없어. ……내 쪽에서 그만 찾아오라고 따돌린 적도 많았다. 그것도 마음대로 안 되더라구. 잊을 만하면 또 술 마시고 와서 인생이 어떻다나, 나 때문에 괴롭다나. 어떡하니, 혼자 지칠 때까지 놔두는 수밖에.

출입문을 바라다본 나는 하마터면 비명을 지를 뻔했다. 유령처럼 들어서는 이는 박 선생님이었다. 그가 입은 미색의 바바리코트가 비에 푹 젖어, 아니, 빗물인지 술인지 그의 온몸에서는 술내가 말도 못하게 났다.

「박 선생님!」

「뭐 하니? 손님 오셨는데 엽차 올리지 않구.」

어느새 언니의 목소리가 낭랑하게 울린다. 깜짝 놀라 뒤를 돌아다보았을 때는 언니는 거짓말처럼 반짝 일어

was that clean in front of me, you know, a woman who'd gone through dozens of men in a bar! Disgusting!

"I tried to turn him away so many times, told him to please stop coming to see me. That didn't work very well, though. When he was completely drunk he'd visit me around the time I thought I'd finally forgotten him. Then, he'd cry about his life, and me, who'd caused him all this misery. So what could I do? I just had to let him be."

When I glance over at our shop entrance, I almost gasp. The person who's entering our shop like a ghost is none other than Mr. Park. His beige raincoat is completely soaked from the rain. No, whatever it is, rain or booze, he reeks of liquor from every pore in his body.

"Mr. Park!" I gasp.

"What are you doing? Why don't you bring a cup of barley tea to our customer?" Sister's voice is clear.

Surprised, I turn around and see her head towards the kitchen. It suddenly feels unreal that she was lying on the sofa just a moment ago. She looks dizzy, and briefly leans on the kitchen doorframe, but other than that, she looks totally normal.

나 주방을 향하는 중이었다. 현기증이 나는지 주방 입구 벽에 잠깐 기대는 것을 제외하고는 언니는 보통 때와 전혀 다름이 없었다.

「아줌마, 여기 찻주전자 불이 꺼져 있잖아요? 손님 오시는데.」

주방 아줌마에게 이르는 언니의 목소리는 그야말로 청명하게 갠, 높은 하늘이다. 보리차 잔을 박 선생님 앞에 놓으면서 나는 나도 모르게 그의 앞자리에 앉아버렸다. 무슨 꿈이라도 꾸는 기분이다. 꿈이 아니고는 모두 이럴 수가 없는 것이다.

「시골에 가신다고 하셨잖아요.」

「내려가지 않았어.」

「그게 무슨 소리예요? 어머니가 얼마나 기다리시겠어요?」

「……형수님이 계시니까. ……나야, 일이 많기도 하고.」

「무슨 일이 많아요? 여기 오는 일요? 아들이 왜 그래요? 작년에도 안 가셨다면서요.」

나도 내가 왜 이러는지 알 수 없었다. 내가 분해서, 몸

"Auntie, look at this! The kettle's not warm. We have a customer."

Sister's voice is as clear as the sky on a good day. After putting the barley tea cup in front of him, I take a seat in front of him without even thinking about it. I feel as if I'm in a dream. This can't be if this isn't a dream.

"Didn't you say you were going to your home village?" I ask.

"I decided not to go."

"What are you talking about? Think about your mother dying to see you again!"

"My sister-in-law can take care of her," he says after a pause. "And besides, I have a lot of work to do, you know."

"What work? You mean, coming here? What kind of a son are you? Didn't you say that you didn't go to see her last year, either?"

I don't know why I'm this way. I'm so upset that I'm trembling. I wasn't this way just a little while ago. Just a few minutes ago I'd hoped that he would return as soon as possible. It was hard for Auntie and me to calm Sister down. But, how could this be? He could have gone to his home village and come back in a day or two? How could he not go at all?

이 와들와들 떨리고 있었다. 조금 전까지만 해도 이렇지 않았다. 박 선생님이 하루바삐 와줄 것을 진짜 고대한 사람이 나였다. 아줌마와 나, 둘의 힘으로 언니를 다잡는다는 게 너무 힘겨웠던 것이 사실이다. 그러나 도대체 이게 말이 되나? 시골에 갔다가 내일 모레, 그때 올라오면 되는 일이지, 아예 내려가지도 않다니. 여자 때문에, 그것도 술집에서 만난 계집 때문에 자기 엄마가 언제 돌아가실지도 모르는데 가보지도 못한다니. 나는 답답해서 가슴이 터질 것만 같다. 힐난하는 듯한 내 말투에 박 선생님이 힘없이 웃는다. 새로 산 우산은 또 어디에다 버렸는지 머리꼭대기부터 푹 젖었다. 양손은 바바리 주머니에 찌른 채 소파에 기대어 앉은 모양이 던져놓은 장작개비 같다. 조는 듯 눈을 껌벅이는 그를 보며 나는 눈물까지 쑥 비어져 나오는 것을 억지로 참는다.

「어머나 사장님, 너무 오랜만이다? 이리 앉으세요. 우리 집하고는 완전히 발 끊으신 줄 알았어.」

다방 문을 밀고 들어서는 세 명의 사내들을 향해 떠는 언니의 호들갑이 유난스럽다.

Just because of a woman, a woman he met at a bar for that matter? Wouldn't it have made more sense to visit his mom who might pass away any moment? I feel so hot and trapped inside that my heart is about to burst. Mr. Park grins listlessly after I scold him. He must have thrown away his new umbrella somewhere. He's soaked from head to toe. The way he sits, leaning on the sofa with his hands in his coat pockets, reminds me of haphazard pile of wood. As I watch him open and close his eyes over and over as if he's dozing off, I try to fight back the tears.

"Wow, Mr. President! How long has it been? Please sit here! I thought you decided not to come to my shop!" Sister fusses over the three men who have just entered the coffee shop.

"You look even prettier today!" they cry, all seeming to enjoying Sister's attention. "Have you just heard some good news? Are you getting married?"

Sister's even cruder than usual. She goes to their table even though they didn't even ask her to. She plays the shameless flirt, brushing her chest against the men's arms. Mr. Park closes his eyes serenely. Can't he hear her?

「오늘따라 마담 얼굴이 확 피었는데? 무슨 좋은 소식 있는 거 아냐? 시집 가?」

언니의 행동은 더욱 천박스럽다. 그들이 따로 부르지도 않았는데 자리에 합석하여, 사내들의 팔에 젖가슴을 비벼가며 갖은 아양을 다 떤다. 박 선생님은 편안히 눈을 감았다. 그는 언니의 저런 코맹맹이 소리를 듣지도 못하는 것일까.

보세요, 언니가 어떤 사람인가. 저런 여자 때문에 부모도 버려요? 정신 좀 차리시라구요.

나는 속으로 그에게 종주먹을 댄다. 그러나 그는 꿈쩍도 하지 않는다. 그의 얼굴에 조금씩 떠오르는 표정은 희한하게도, 편안하고 만족스런 행복감 같은 것이다. 어머니에게 내려갈 것을 포기해야만 했던 불효자로서의 자책감 따위는 아예 없다. 언니에게 무언가를 요구하는 갈망의 표정도 아니다. 언니의 코맹맹이 소리를 자장가처럼 들으며 평안함을 얻고 있는, 도무지 이해할 수 없는 화평한 얼굴이다. 세상에 부러울 것 없는, 천진난만한 어린아이의 얼굴.

「어머, 점잖으신 분이 왜 이래? 건드리지 말아요!」

Look at what kind of a woman she is! You deserted your mother for a woman like that? Come to your senses!

I rebuke him in my mind. He, of course, doesn't respond. His face shows, incredibly, a sense of comfort and happiness, a sort of satisfaction. There's no trace of any feelings of guilt for giving up on visiting his mother. His face doesn't show any sort of yearning, a demand for Sister, either. It's a peaceful face, comfortable in the presence of Sister's lilting, throaty flirts as if she were singing a lullaby. He has a face that's impossible for me to understand. A face like an innocent child. Not a care in the world.

"Oh, no! A gentleman like you! What kind of behavior is this? Don't touch!" Sister is still giggling and playing the shameless flirt. As Sister continues to coo and laugh, Mr. Park's face gradually begins to change. His face turns mischievous, as if the man placing his hand on Sister's waist is not the man at another table, but Mr. Park himself.

"Goodness! Where's your hand going? Look at your friend looking at you!" Sister giggles again.

This can't be Mr. Park. His face shows not a trace of the clean, clear, and melancholy poet. He looks

언니의 자지러지는 웃음소리와 함께 그의 표정이 서서히 바뀌기 시작한다. 언니의 허리에 손을 감는 사람이 저만치 떨어져 앉은 사내가 아니라, 마치 박 선생님 당사자인 것처럼, 그의 얼굴 표정이 짓궂게 일그러지고 있다.

「어머머, 얻다 손을 넣어? 옆엣 분 쳐다보는 거 봐요!」

이건 분명 박 선생님이 아니다. 정갈하고 맑고 처연한 시인의 것이 아닌, 술 취한 사내, 여자의 유방과 아랫도리를 지분대며 능갈치는 치한의 표정이다. 여자를 깔축없이 짓뭉개며 자신의 정욕을 채우는 만용의 얼굴. 헤벌어진 입술 틈으로 나지막이 흘러나오는 짐승의 소리. 이게 다 무슨 일이란 말인가. 나는 그만 왕 울어버리고 싶다. 언니도, 언니도 그렇다. 아무에게나 몸을 맡기고 히히덕대는, 적어도 저 정도의 싸구려 여자는 아니었다. 도도하고 시 건방진, 웬만한 사내들은 상대도 하지 않는 콧대 높기로 유명한 자칭 일류 마담이었다. 술기운이 아직 떨어지지 않은 것일까. 온갖 유치한 짓거리를 스스로 벌이는 와중에도 힐끔힐끔 이쪽을 살피는 언니의 속마음은 또 무엇이란 말인가.

like a common drunk, a pervert who'd grab at a woman's breasts and bottom. He has the face of brute, the face of someone who'd ruthlessly rape a woman. There's a low animal moaning coming out of his mouth, which is slightly agape. What the hell's happening? I feel like crying.

Sister. As for Sister, she's never behaved this cheaply, either, giggling whenever one of those nobodies touches her. She's always been a self-styled first-rate hostess, proud and arrogant, a woman who'd ignore ordinary guys. Is she still drunk? What is she thinking when she shoots glances in this direction and then acts like this at the same time?

"Sir!" I call Mr. Park as if to challenge him.

He doesn't respond, though. I can't believe how despicable his behavior is. If he likes her so much, if he enjoys her superficiality and capriciousness so much, then why not just take her to bed like a man?

"Sir, please say something!"

I get up halfway and shake him rudely by his shoulder. As if waking from his sleep, he opens his eyes slowly.

"What? What's the matter?"

「선생님.」

나는 마치 싸움을 거는 심정으로 박 선생님을 불렀다. 그러나 그는 아무 반응이 없다. 그의 태도가 이렇게 가증스러울 수가 없다. 그렇게 언니가 좋으면, 천박하고 요사스런 언니의 행동이 그렇게 즐거우면 떳떳하게 품고 자면 되지 않는가 말이다.

「선생님, 말 좀 하세요.」

나는 엉거주춤 일어나 왈살스레 그의 어깨를 흔든다. 잠에서 깨어나듯 그가 천천히 눈을 뜬다.

「……왜, 무슨 일 있어?」

「언니는 좋겠어요.」

나는 나도 모르게 입에서 쏟아져 나온 말에 당황한다.

「뭐가?」

박 선생님이 내게 묻는다. 나는 되도록 그의 얼굴을 보지 않고 아무렇지도 않은 듯 재빨리 말을 잇는다.

「최사장님이라고…… 부동산하는 분인데 돈이 많은가 봐요. 그분하고 결혼하시기로 했대요.」

박 선생님이 빙긋 웃는 듯하더니 또다시 눈을 감아버린다. 나는 또 가슴이 콱 막힌다.

"Sister must be happy," I say. And I feel embarrassed by what I've just unconsciously said.

"Why?" Mr. Park asks me.

Avoiding his eyes, I pretend to casually mention, "President Choe... I hear he's a rich man who owns a real estate agency. She might marry him."

Mr. Park seems to grin and then closes his eyes again. I feel my heart is going to burst again.

"Do you know how much you annoyed Sister? You follow her around as if you're her guardian! And now she's treating you unfairly. Do you know what kind of a woman she is? After we close the shop at night, she goes with other guys as if nothing's the matter. She even takes them to her house. You're the only one who doesn't know, because you leave early. I'm telling you the truth. Ask Auntie!"

"Yun-hi," he stops and then continues after a pause, "Please just leave me alone."

Although he is completely aware I'm staring at him, he just closes his eyes again. There's no trace of any dark feelings in his face. It's not like he doesn't believe what I'm telling him, just that he doesn't care a bit about any of it. So, then... Is their love a spiritual love, a love that has nothing to do

「언니가 선생님을 얼마나 귀찮아한다구요? 보호자도 아니면서 맨날 따라붙는다고. 선생님만 억울하다니까요. 언니가 어떤 여잔 줄 아세요? 밤에 영업 끝나면 아무렇지도 않게 사내들하고 어울려요. 언니 집에도 끌고 가구요. 박 선생님만 모르신다구요. 일찍 가시니까. 진짜예요, 아줌마한테도 물어보세요.」

「윤희씨, 나…… 이대로 좀 앉아 있을게.」

내가 빤히 쳐다보고 있음을 알면서도, 그는 다시 눈을 감는다. 그의 얼굴에는 동요되는 기색이라곤 전혀 없다. 내가 고자질한 것을 믿지 않는다기보다는, 이미 그런 일들은 둘 사이에 문제조차 될 수 없다는 표정이다. 그러니까…… 육체를 뛰어넘은 정신, 정신의 사랑을 한다는 말인가? 그저 서로 곁에 있어주기만 하면 바랄 것이 없다? 그러면 조금 전까지 그의 얼굴에 서렸던 야비한 수컷의 표정은 무엇이란 말인가. 언니의 저 간드러지는 요부의 웃음을, 나는 또 어떻게 이해해야 옳단 말인가.

나는 하릴없이 자리에서 일어난다. 다방 문을 열고 바깥으로 나선다. 갑자기 내가 어리석다는 생각이 든다.

with body? So, they don't want anything more than to be around each other? If so, then, what was that filthy look I just saw in his face? Also, how am I supposed to interpret Sister's coquettish giggles?

I get up, helpless. I open the coffee shop door and leave. Suddenly, I feel so stupid. Sister and Mr. Park are tied together forever! No matter how incomprehensible their feelings are to others, whether they themselves understand them or not, their love is just there like their ultimate fate. It doesn't matter the conditions or the forms!

The rain doesn't stop all day. There's water, water, water everywhere, in the sky, on the road, inside the trashcans on the street. Hyeon-su and Miss Yang are walking towards me under one umbrella. Seeing me walking in the rain without an umbrella, Hyeon-su clearly looks embarrassed. I can see it even under the shade of an umbrella.

"Hi, Yun-hi! What's up? Why are you walking around like this in the rain? Did you just get dumped?" Hyeon-su says.

"I did. You must be happy, Miss Yang! You've got a real nice boyfriend there."

Although I can barely fight back my tears, I make a desperate effort to speak proudly to Hyeon-su.

언니와 박 선생님은 한운명이다! 옆사람들이 아무리 이해하지 못한다 해도, 당사자들조차 이해하지 못한다 하더라도. 사랑은 조건이나 형식을 뛰어넘어 그냥 운명처럼 거기 있는 것이다!

비는 하루 종일 그어댄다. 하늘도, 땅도, 길가의 쓰레기통도 온통 물, 물 구덕이다. 현수와 미스 양이 한 우산을 쓰고 걸어오는 중이다. 비를 맞으며 걷는 내 모습을 보고 현수가 당황하는 품이 어두운 우산 속에서도 역력하다.

「윤희 아냐? 웬일이냐? 실연당한 여자처럼 비는 죽죽 맞고.」

「실연당했어. 미스 양은 좋겠네, 좋은 애인 있어서.」

울음이 터져나오기 직전인데 그래도 난 현수에게는 결사적으로 당당하게 말한다. 쳐다보는 미스 양의 눈초리가 헬기죽하다. 그들 옆을 그대로 지나친다.

비를 맞으니 한결 마음이 편하다. 머리도 옷도 푹 젖지만 덕분에 마음도 푹 젖는다. 하늘은 정말 엄청 많은 눈물을 가졌다. 어두운 밤이라는 사실도 참 다행이다. 허청허청 아무렇게나 걸어도 흉보는 사람이 없다. 가로등

Miss Yang looks at me a bit sideways. I just pass them by.

Getting wet under the rain, I feel much better. My hair's wet, my clothes are wet, but my heart feels wet, too. The sky really is full of tears tonight. I'm glad it's dark out. Nobody says anything about me, even though I'm walking aimlessly. Whenever I pass under a circle of light from a street lamp, I seem to see the face of Mr. Park, who clearly must have been enjoying Sister's behavior.

"Yun-hi! You're something else! If you talk like that in front of Miss Yang, how do you think that'll make her feel?" Hyeon-su is suddenly beside me and covers me with his umbrella. He tries to control his breathing; he must have run after me.

"What are you talking about?"

"When did I dump you? What are you talking about?" he says too loudly, clearly very excited. Come to think of it, Hyeon-su, Auntie, they all deserve pity. I feel like linking my arm with his for the first time.

"If you hadn't been so proud and standoffish, do you think I'd have gone out with someone like Miss Yang? Well—it's true that your pride makes you attractive."

불빛의 동그란 원을 맞고 지나보낼 때마다, 언니의 교태를 즐기며 앉아 있을 박 선생님의 얼굴이 환히 보이는 듯하다. 박 선생님도, 언니도 참 측은한 사람들이다.

「참, 윤희 너 이제 보니 보통 애가 아니다. 미스 양 앞에서 그렇게 노골적으로 그러면, 걔가 뭐가 되냐?」

어느덧 뒤쫓아온 현수가 애써 숨을 고르며 우산을 씌워준다.

「……내가 어쨌게?」

「내가 언제 너를 딱지 놓았냐? 실연이니 뭐니 거창하게 나오게.」

그는 신이 나서 떠벌리기 시작한다. 따지고 보면 현수도, 주방 아줌마도 모두 불쌍한 사람들이다. 처음으로 나는 그의 팔짱을 끼고 싶다는 생각이 든다.

「네가 그렇게 톡톡거리지만 않으면 내가 미스 양 같은 애하고 어울려 다니겠냐? 하긴 그게 네 매력이지만.」

현수가 마음 좋게 히히 웃는다. 비닐로 벽을 친 포장마차 옆을 지나는데 젓가락 박자에 맞춘 유행가가 흘러나온다. 유치하기 짝이 없는, 노인네들의 사랑타령이라고만 생각했던 뽕짝조 노래가 오늘따라 가슴 깊은 곳을

Hyeon-su smiles good-naturedly. We pass by the plastic wall of a covered wagon. I can hear a popular tune coming from it, accompanied by a chopstick beat. The trotting tune, which, I have always thought, was love music for old people, suddenly touches me and I can feel it echoing through me like the sound of the Emille Bell on New Year's Eve. Hyeon-su's warm and irregular breath touches my earlobe. I'm a little stunned, as if I'm drunk with hard liquor, but Hyeon-su seems terribly anxious.

"I wanna get wet," I say, pushing his arm away, which was forcing me under the umbrella.

"Yun-hi, are you still angry? Are you upset?"

Still, Hyeon-su folds his umbrella and holds out his hand.

The trees in the park look entirely different from how they looked during the day. The green leaves of early summer look more mature and firmer because they're wet.

"The trees look as if they're breathing in fresh air for the first time in a long while," I say.

"Naturally. Could dust even stay on the leaves with this much rain?"

Although, on the one hand, I feel empty and bit-

치고는 마치 제야의 에밀레 종소리처럼 멀리멀리 퍼져 간다. 현수의 훗훗하고 불규칙한 숨결이 귓가에 닿는 다. 독한 술에 취한 것처럼 먹먹한 내 기분과는 달리, 현 수는 자기대로 잔뜩 긴장하여 가슴이 설레는 모양이다.

「난 그냥 비 맞을 거야.」

억지로 우산 속으로 끌어들이는 현수의 팔을 조용히 잡아뗀다.

「윤희 너, 아직도 화났냐? 분이 안 풀리냐?」

말은 그렇게 하면서도 현수 역시 우산을 접어 손에 쥔다.

공원에 들어찬 나무들은 낮과는 또 천양지차로 보인 다. 초여름의 푸른 잎새들이 빗물에 젖으니 훨씬 더 성 숙하고 믿음직해 보인다.

「나무들이 오랜만에 시원하게 숨을 쉬는 것 같애.」

「당연하지, 임마. 비가 그렇게 왔는데 이파리의 먼지 인들 남아나겠냐.」

허전하고 쓸쓸한 한편으로 나는 어쨌든 행복하다는 생각이 든다. 사랑이라는 낱말의 실체를 오늘밤 처음 본 것 같은 느낌. 그리고 사랑이란, 희망이라곤 전혀 없

ter, I feel happy at any rate. I feel as if I've seen what love really is for the first time tonight. Love is something like a heavenly blessing gently descending on the foreheads of hopeless lovers to cover their wounds.

"Yun-hi, you're taller!"

Perhaps the rainy season is beginning. The deep scent of sap wafts through the air from the trees. I don't shake Hyeon-su's arm from off my shoulders. Love, hopelessly! Lovers facing each other with eyes closed! The deepest truth is visible only when you close your eyes. Love, hopelessly!

Translated by Jeon Seung-hee

는 상처투성이 연인들의 이마에 슬며시 그어주는 하늘의 축복 같은 것.

「윤희야, 너 이제 보니 키 많이 컸다?」

본격적인 장마가 시작되려는 모양인지 나무들에서는 진한 수액의 냄새가 난다. 내 어깨에 두르는 현수의 팔을 나는 구태여 뿌리치지 않는다. 사랑하라, 희망 없이. 눈감은 채 마주 선 연인들이여. 가장 깊은 진실은 눈을 감아야 보이나니. 사랑하라, 희망 없이, 사랑하라.

『사랑하라, 희망 없이』, 민음사, 1994

해설

Afterword

눈감은 채 마주선 연인들

이경재 (문학평론가)

    윤영수의「사랑하라, 희망 없이」는 도시 변두리에 있는 친척 언니의 다방에서 차심부름을 하는 18세의 윤희가 사랑의 열병을 앓으며 성장하는 과정을 담고 있는 소설이다. 도시 변두리의 다방을 주요한 배경으로 한 이 소설에는 하층민의 고단한 삶이 적지 않은 분량으로 등장한다. 폐가처럼 허름한 집, 새로 생긴 슈퍼에 손님을 빼앗기는 동네가게의 할머니, 현수의 고물 오토바이, 사창가에 팔려간 젊은 여인, 찻잔 하나 깨뜨렸다는 이유로 쏟아지는 욕지거리, 과자를 훔쳐 먹은 아들을 때려 장애를 만든 어머니 등이 윤영수 특유의 꼼꼼한 솜씨를 통해 정밀하게 재현되고 있다.

Lovers Facing Each Other with Their Eyes Closed

Lee Kyung-jae (literary critic)

Yun Young-su's "Love, Hopelessly" is a classic bildungsroman, a journey for eighteen-year-old girl Yun-hi traveling through the fever and forays of first love. Yun-hi works as a waitress at a coffee shop run by her cousin, whom Yun-hi calls "Sister," on the outskirts of an unnamed city. Set in this backdrop of a coffee shop, this novella features the lives of a tired, battered lower class rather extensively. A dilapidated, almost abandoned-looking house, an ancient neighborhood store owner constantly losing her customers to a newly opened supermarket, Hyeon-su's old motorcycle, a young, former prostitute, a girl showered with curses for

그러나 아무래도 이 작품의 초점은 여성이 여러 가지 연애를 직간접적으로 체험하며 한 명의 성인 여성으로 성장하는 과정에 놓여 있다. 이때의 성장은 세상에 영향을 줄 수 있는 현실적 힘을 갖게 되거나 세상을 꿰뚫어 보는 지적 능력을 갖게 되는 것을 의미하지 않는다. 오히려 본래의 자신은 대단한 능력이 없는 결핍된 존재임을, 즉 자신이 거세된 존재라는 것을 인정하게 되는 정신분석학적인 개념의 성장에 가깝다.

처음 윤희는 세상이 온통 자신을 바라보며 또 자신을 좋아한다는 착각 속에 살아간다. 윤희의 옆에는 두 명의 남자가 있는데, 한 명은 언니의 연인인 박일도라는 학원 선생이고 다른 한 명은 같은 또래로 신문 배달을 하는 현수이다. 윤희는 "무식"한 현수가 자신을 열렬히 사랑한다고 생각하며, 현수와 데이트를 하기도 하는 디피점의 미스 양은 자기와는 비교도 안 되는 사람이라고 평가 절하한다. 나아가 윤희는 "유식"한 박 선생이 얼마 가지 않아 자신의 애인이 될 것이라 확신한다. 윤희는 열네 살이 많은 박 선생이야말로 술집여자인 언니가 아니라 자신의 애인이 되어야 한다고 생각하는 것이다. 윤희는 한동안 박 선생이 가지고 다니던 미색의 플라스

failing menial tasks like breaking a single cup, and a mother who beats her own son to the point of debilitation for stealing—all of the members of this haunted, motley crew are skillfully represented through Yun Young-su's superb descriptive skills.

The novella focuses, however, on the process of growing up of a young woman through the direct and indirect experiences of various love affairs. Growing up here does not mean acquiring the real powers to influence the world or intellectual power to penetrate it. On the contrary, Yun's novella recognizes the lack of individual agency in so many realities, a kind of castration for so many, to describe it psychoanalytically.

At the outset of Yun's work, Yun-hi seems to live in an illusionary world in which everyone around her seems to be looking at and enamored of her. There are two central male figures in Yun-hi's life —Park Il-do, a private institute teacher and her cousin's lover, and Hyeon-su, a newspaper delivery boy around Yun-hi's age. Yun-hi believes that the "ignorant" Hyeon-su loves her dearly and Miss Yang, who occasionally goes out with Hyeon-su, is nothing compared to herself. In addition, Yun-hi is sure that the supposedly more intelligent Mr. Park

틱 손잡이가 달린 박쥐우산을 가지고 다니며 행복해 하는데, 이 우산의 손잡이는 박 선생의 남근을 의미하는 동시에 윤희가 자신이 가지고 있다고 생각하는 상상 속의 남근을 의미하는 기호라고 할 수 있다. 그러나 자신에 대한 이러한 과도한 가치부여는 곧 깨어질 운명이다. 윤희는 언니와 박 선생의 사랑을 지켜보며 세상은 자신이 쉽게 의미를 파악할 만큼 간단하지 않으며, 그 복잡하고 불투명한 세상의 중심은 자신이 아니라는 사실을 깨닫는다. 자신은 "유식"한 존재가 아니라 "무식"한 존재임을 알게 된 것이다.

공통 감각에 비추어 볼 때 가장 불가해한 사랑을 나누는 것은 언니와 박 선생이다. 언니는 고등학교 2학년 때 상경하여 사창가에 팔려갔다. 휴가 나온 군인이었던 박 선생은 그곳에서 언니를 처음 만났으며, 그 이후로 계속 해서 언니와 인연을 이어오고 있다. 박 선생은 하루도 빠짐없이 다방에 오지만 언니에게 특별한 행동을 하지도 않으며, 언니 역시 박 선생이 있거나 없거나 그대로 손님을 맞는다. 언니는 평소에 박 선생에게 쌀쌀한 편이며, 윤희는 언니가 박 선생을 "발가락의 때만큼도 여기지 않"는다고 생각한다. 그러나 하루도 빠짐없

will become her lover soon. She is sure that Mr. Park, a man fourteen years her senior, should be her lover, not her older cousin or Sister, as Yun-hi calls her, considering her cousin is nothing but a long-time barmaid. Yun-hi happily holds on to Mr. Park's black umbrella, its ivory-colored handle possibly signifying a sort of phallic element of Mr. Park's, one which Yun-hi believes that she owns. This excessive sense of self-value, however, soon to collapses. Seeing the masochistic love between Mr. Park and her cousin, Yun-hi realizes that the world is more complicated than she can comprehend; she is not the center of this new complicated, opaque world. She realizes that it is she that is truly "ignorant" in the ways of the world.

The most inscrutable love affair in "Love Hopelessly" exists between Yun-hi's elder cousin and Mr. Park. Yun-hi-s cousin, a high school dropout and Seoul migrant, originally found her way in the city as a young prostitute. It was during this time when Mr. Park met her for the first time while on compulsory military service leave. Since then, although Mr. Park comes to the coffee shop everyday, he nearly ignores her, even while always acutely aware of her presence. Her cousin, in turn,

이 다방에 오던 박 선생이 형수 혼자서 수발해온 어머님이 편찮으셔서 며칠 동안 시골에 다녀오겠다고 하자 언니는 그때부터 병적인 반응을 보이기 시작한다. "잘됐어요. 축하해요. 이제 다시는 여기 안 와도 돼요"라고 말하기도 하고, "빌어먹을 인간. 지겨워, 지겨워"라는 소리를 하기도 한다. 그러한 모습을 보며 윤희는 처음으로 박 선생만 언니를 짝사랑하는 것이 아니라 언니도 박 선생을 좋아하는 것일지 모른다고 생각한다.

그토록 당당하던 언니는 박 선생이 보이지 않자 손님과 싸우며 "신세타령에 지친 술 취한 작부"로 변모한다. 다방 문을 잠그지도 못하게 하던 언니의 뜻이 전달된 듯, 박 선생은 온몸에서 술내를 풍기며 "유령" 같은 모습으로 나타난다. 결국 박 선생은 언니 때문에 시골에는 내려가 보지도 못하고 다방에 돌아온 것이다. 그러나 박 선생은 불효자로서의 자책감도 언니에게 무언가를 요구하는 갈망도 없이 "편안하고 만족스런 행복감"을 얼굴에 드러낸다. 이러한 모습을 지켜보며, 윤희는 "언니와 박 선생님은 한운명이다! 옆 사람들이 아무리 이해하지 못한다 해도, 당사자들조차 이해하지 못한다 하더라도. 사랑은 조건이나 형식을 뛰어넘어 그냥 운명처

seems almost entirely indifferent to his presence, usually acting so coldly towards him. Yun-hi remarks Sister "doesn't think he's worth the dirt between her toes."

Their temperaments, however, reverse when Mr. Park informs Yun-hi's cousin that he will be visiting his sick mother in the countryside for a few days. Yun-hi's cousin reacts perversely: "That's wonderful. Congratulations! You don't have to drop by here any more," she exclaims, as well as "I'm sick and tired of him." Finally witnessing these reactions, Yun-hi begins to realize that Mr. Park's love for her cousin might not be as unrequited as she had once believed. Furthermore, Yun-hi's cousin, who once seemed so proud, picks a fight with her customers and changes into "just a drunken prostitute, exhausted after her tale of woe, prostrate." Then, as if Sister's desires—also expressed in her insistence on not locking the gate of the coffee shop—somehow found a way to materialize, Mr. Park shows up at the coffee shop "like a ghost," and reeking of liquor. Aborting his countryside visit for Yun-hi's cousin, he returns to the coffee shop. Yet, Mr. Park shows neither a sense of guilt for failing in his filial obligations nor a sense of yearn-

럼 거기 있는 것이다!"라는 깨달음에 도달한다.

윤희가 '사랑은 조건이나 형식을 뛰어넘어 그냥 운명처럼 거기 있는 것'이라는 진실을 깨닫는 데에는 주방 아줌마도 큰 영향을 미쳤다. 왼쪽 눈이 씰그러진 주방 아줌마는 한마디로 "진국"이다. 그런 아줌마는 새 여자와 살림을 차린 남편에게 월말이 되면 꼬박꼬박 생활비를 건넨다. 사실 주방 아줌마는 사주단자만 받았을 뿐 남편이라는 자와 혼인 신고도 한 바 없는 사이이다. 상식적으로는 말이 되지 않는 일을 주방 아줌마는 사랑이라는 이름으로 담담히 받아들인다. 그러한 아줌마를 보며 윤희는 "자기 남자를 자기 방식대로 사랑"하고 있는 것이라는 결론에 이른다.

결코 세상은 자기를 중심으로 움직이지 않는다는 것을, 이 세상은 자신이 모르는 것들로 가득하다는 것을 알게 된 윤희는 평소 그토록 경멸하고 무시하던 현수를 찾아간다. 윤희는 처음으로 현수의 팔짱을 끼고 싶다는 생각이 들었던 것인데, 이러한 욕망은 자신이 "무식"한 존재이며 사랑이란 "희망이라곤 전혀 없는 상처투성이 연인들의 이마에 슬며시 그어주는 하늘의 축복 같은 것"이라는 것을 깨달은 데서 비롯된다. 이 작품의 마지

ing for Yun-hi's cousin. He seems to have "a sense of comfort and happiness, a sort of satisfaction," prompting Yun-hi to realize that "Sister and Mr. Park are tied together forever! No matter how incomprehensible their feelings are to others, whether they themselves understand them or not, their love is just there like their ultimate fate. It doesn't matter the conditions or the forms!"

Yun-hi's realization that love is "just there like their ultimate fate" regardless of the conditions or forms is also indebted greatly to her Auntie, the cook who works at the kitchen of the coffee shop. Auntie, with her crooked left eye, is "the real thing," handing her husband an allowance every month despite her questionable marriage status and her husband's open disregard for her. Her marital status, in fact, stands as having never legally registered—although she "received the formal letter to the house of the fiancée where the four pillars of the bridegroom-to-be are written." Auntie calmly accepts what does not ordinarily make sense in the name of love. Once again, Yun-hi realizes that Auntie as well loves her man in her own way.

At this point, upon accepting her position in the world and her own ignorance, Yun-hi finally ac-

막은 강력한 메시지를 전달하는 잠언풍의 "사랑하라, 희망 없이. 눈감은 채 마주 선 연인들이여. 가장 깊은 진실은 눈을 감아야 보이나니. 사랑하라, 희망 없이, 사랑하라"라는 문장으로 끝난다.

가장 깊은 진실을 보기 위해서 눈을 감으라는 말이다. 눈이란 아주 오래전부터 인간의 이성을 상징하는 대표적 신체부위가 아니었던가? 그렇다면 사랑이란 더 넓게 보자면 인간들 사이의 관계란 결코 합리성에 바탕한 이성 따위로 이루어지는 것이 아니라는 것, 오히려 그러한 이성적 판단을 넘어선 운명적 받아들임 속에서만 가능하다는 것을 '눈감은 채 마주 선 연인들'의 형상은 우리에게 알려주고 있는 것이다.

cepts Hyeon-su, whom she has despised and ignored throughout almost the entire narrative. For
the first time, Yun-hi finds herself not minding Hyeon-su's arm around her shoulders. She comes to
the conclusion that she is "ignorant" and that "love
is something like a heavenly blessing gently descending on the foreheads of hopeless lovers to
cover their wounds." The novella ends with prov-
erb-like phrases: "Love, hopelessly! Lovers facing
each other with eyes closed! The deepest truth is
visible only when you close your eyes. Love,
hopelessly!"

Ultimately, "Love, Hopelessly" asks us to close
our eyes to see the deepest truth. And aren't eyes,
perhaps the most representative of our bodily or-
gans, symbolic of human reason? Thus, the image
of "lovers facing each other with eyes closed"
seems to propose that love, or in a more broad
sense, human relationships, fall outside the bound-
aries of reason; they are a matter of fateful accep-
tance beyond rational judgment.

비평의 목소리

Critical Acclaim

우선 그녀의 문학에 자전적 성격이 아주 희박하다는 데 주목해야 한다. 말하자면 그녀는 오랜만에 등장한 정통파 소설가다. 이 소설집만 해도 그녀는 얼마나 다양한 인물들 속에 숨어 있는가? 자기 이야기도 남의 이야기처럼, 남의 이야기도 자기 이야기처럼 풀어내는 능갈침, 그것은 단순한 재주를 넘어서 진정한 소설가의 원력이기도 하다. 그런데 그녀의 작품들을 찬찬히 들여다보노라면 자신의 경험적 구체성을 소중히 갈무리한 결과로서 나타난 여성적 관점이 맥맥하다.

최원식

It is noteworthy that Yun's literature is rarely autobiographical. In other words, she is one of the first truly authentic fiction writers to emerge on our literary scene in a long while. In this current short story collection, behind how many of her various characters is Yun hiding? This talent to spin one's stories as if they were other's—and vice versa—is far more than only one of her many basic skills; it is, in fact, the source of creativity for any true fiction writer. And, when we examine her works closely, we can clearly see the presence of a woman's perspective, the products of cherished personal experiences.

Choe Won-sik

윤영수는 기법이든 주제든 모든 면에서 겉치레적이고 일회적인 것, 그리고 감정적인 도발의 측면으로 지향하고 있는 최근의 젊은 소설가들의 세계에 비해 훨씬 믿음직한 소설의 세계를 구축하고 있는 작가로 평가할 수 있을 것이다. 뿐만 아니라 서투르게 초장르의 세계로 몰입하는 최근의 상황에서도 나름대로 중편의 세계에 대한 군건한 장르적 이해 위에서 행해지는 윤영수의 소설은 중편양식의 재발견이라는 측면에서도 소중한 소설적 성과라 할 수 있다.

　　　　　　　　　　　　　　　　　　　　　　김경수

　　윤영수는 부정성의 완강한 의식 속에서 보다 나은 것의 가능성을 붙잡으려는 시선 이외에 순수한 아름다움이나 위안은 더 이상 존재하지 않는다는 사실을 깨닫고 보다 나은 것의 가능성을 꼼꼼하게 찾아내어 그야말로 문학적으로 누벼낸다. 한국문학의 짧지 않은 역사 속에서 좀처럼 볼 수 없었던 일대 장관이다.

　　　　　　　　　　　　　　　　　　　　　　류보선

　　윤영수 소설을 연옥이라고 부르는 것은 새삼스러운

In comparison to many young novelists these days, more oriented to the superficial, the disposable, and the sensationalist, Yun Young-su has been busy fashioning her own unique, far more concrete fictional world. Additionally, Yun's rediscovery of novellas, based on a grounded understanding of the novella genre, is a precious literary achievement in this current literary scene where writers hastily rush to a seemingly genre-less world.

Kim Gyeong-su

Yun seems keenly aware that there exists no pure beauty or comfort other than the ones that spring from our own perspectives searching for better possibilities, all while firmly rooted in an awareness of this present adverse reality. Yun carefully looks for better possibilities and weaves them together in literature. Her works offer a magnificent spectacle rare in a rather lengthy Korean literary history.

Ryu Bo-seon

If I were to call Yun Young-su's works a kind of Purgatory, that's nothing new. But, let me add one

.

일이 아니다. 그러나 윤영수 소설이 연옥인 이유를 하나만 더 보충하자. 윤영수 소설은 비단 인간에 대한 최소한의 예의를 망각한 사람들이 모여 사는 곳이라는 의미에서만이 아니라, 그곳이 견뎌내야 하는 곳이라는 의미에서 연옥이다. 소설 속 인물들은 시험대 위에 서 있다. 이들은 시험을 통과하여 천국으로 가거나 실패하여 지옥으로 떨어지게 될 것이다. 이들의 견딤은 윤리적이며 다분히 종말론적이다.

정영훈

more reason for giving her works this name. The world of Yun's works is a kind of Purgatory not only because they seem to occupy a space where characters who've thrown away their basic human decency must learn to live with one another, but also because it is where they must endure. Her characters stand in front of a testing board. They would either go to Heaven or Hell, depending on the results of their tests. Their endurance is both ethical and eschatological.

Jeong Yeong-hun

윤영수

1952년 서울 종로구 동숭동에서 아버지 윤지중과 어머니 이기남의 2남 2녀 중 막내로 출생하였다. 본명은 윤영순이며 경기여중과 경기여고를 졸업하였다. 고등학교 시절 영세를 받았고, 천주교명은 로사리아이다. 1975년 서울대학교 역사교육과를 졸업한 후 여의도 중학교에 부임하였고, 같은 해 이대용과 결혼하였다. 1979년에는 대방여자중학교로 전근을 갔고, 1980년 교직을 그만두었다. 1987년 우연히 문예진흥원 소설 강좌를 듣게 된 것을 계기로 소설 습작을 시작하였다. 서른여덟 살이던 1990년 《현대소설》에 단편 「생태관찰」이 신인상을 받으며 등단했다. 병자, 불구자, 건달, 장애인, 여성 등 한국 사회에서 소외된 사람들의 이야기와 붕괴 직전에 놓인 가족 관계 등을 주로 다루어왔다. 1990년대에 큰 주목을 받아 "우리 소설계에 있어 하나의 희망의 지렛대"(우찬제)라거나 "최근 우리 문학이 거둔 최대의 수확의 하나"(최원식)라는 극찬을 받았다. 이후에도 활발한 활동으로 『자린고비의 죽음을 애도함』『내 여자

Yun Young-su

Yun Young-su was born as Yun Yeong-sun, the
last of four children between Yun Ji-jung and Lee
Gi-nam in Seoul in 1952. She graduated from
Kyunggi Middle and High Schools, and was baptized as a Catholic during high school (baptized
name: Rosaria). Yun graduated from Seoul National
University College of Education with a major in
history education. In 1975, she began teaching at
Yeouido Middle School and married Lee Dae-yong.
She quit teaching in 1980, and began her first at-
tempts at writing in 1987 after taking a course on
novels at the Korea Arts & Culture Education Service. Yun made her literary debut at the age of
thirty-eight in 1990 when she won the *Hyeondae
Soseol* New Writer's Award with her short story
"Ecological Observation." Throughout her career as
a writer, Yun has focused on the lives of the mar-
ginalized in Korean society, including the sick, the
disabled, disenfranchised youth, women, and fami-
lies on the verge of a collapse. Her works have
been critically acclaimed since the 1990s, garnering

213

친구의 귀여운 연애』『귀가도』등 여러 권의 소설집을 출판하였고 각종 문학상을 받았다. 1997년 「착한 사람 문성현」으로 제30회 한국일보문학상을, 2008년 소설집 『내 안의 황무지』로 제3회 남촌문학상을, 같은 해 소설집 『소설 쓰는 밤』으로 제23회 만해문학상을 수상하였다.

high praises like "a lever of hope in the world of the Korean novel (U Chan-je)" and "one of the greatest harvests of recent Korean literature (Choi Won-sik)." Her published works include *Love, Hopelessly* (1994), *Good Man Mun Seong-hyeon* (1997), *A Dirge on Jaringobi's Death* (1998), *Writing Novel at Night* (2006), *My Girl Friend's Cute Love Affair* (2007), *Wasteland in Me* (2007), and *Their Ways Home* (2011). Yun has been honored with *the Hankook Ilbo* Literary Award in 1997, the Namchon Literary Award in 2008, and the Manhae Literary Award in 2008.

번역 **전승희** Translated by Jeon Seung-hee

전승희는 서울대학교와 하버드대학교에서 영문학과 비교문학으로 박사 학위를 받았으며, 현재 하버드대학교 한국학 연구소의 연구원으로 재직하며 아시아 문예 계간지 《ASIA》 편집위원으로 활동 중이다. 현대 한국문학 및 세계문학을 다룬 논문을 다수 발표했으며, 바흐친의 『장편소설과 민중언어』, 제인 오스틴의 『오만과 편견』 등을 공역했다. 1988년 한국여성연구소의 창립과 《여성과 사회》의 창간에 참여했고, 2002년부터 보스턴 지역 피학대 여성을 위한 단체인 '트랜지션하우스' 운영에 참여해 왔다. 2006년 하버드대학교 한국학 연구소에서 '한국 현대사와 기억'을 주제로 한 워크숍을 주관했다.

Jeon Seung-hee is a member of the Editorial Board of *ASIA*, and a Fellow at the Korea Institute, Harvard University. She received a Ph.D. in English Literature from Seoul National University and a Ph.D. in Comparative Literature from Harvard University. She has presented and published numerous papers on modern Korean and world literature. She is also a co-translator of Mikhail Bakhtin's *Novel and the People's Culture* and Jane Austen's *Pride and Prejudice*. She is a founding member of the Korean Women's Studies Institute and of the biannual Women's Studies' journal *Women and Society* (1988), and she has been working at 'Transition House,' the first and oldest shelter for battered women in New England. She organized a workshop entitled "The Politics of Memory in Modern Korea" at the Korea Institute, Harvard University, in 2006. She also served as an advising committee member for the Asia-Africa Literature Festival in 2007 and for the POSCO Asian Literature Forum in 2008.

감수 **데이비드 윌리엄 홍** Edited by David William Hong

데이비드 윌리엄 홍은 미국 일리노이주 시카고에서 태어났다. 일리노이대학교에서 영문학을, 뉴욕대학교에서 영어교육을 공부했다. 지난 2년간 서울에 거주하면서 처음으로 한국인과 아시아계 미국인 문학에 깊이 몰두할 기회를 가졌다. 현재 뉴욕에서 거주하며 강의와 저술 활동을 한다.

David William Hong was born in 1986 in Chicago, Illinois. He studied English Literature at the University of Illinois and English Education at New York University. For the past two years, he lived in Seoul, South Korea, where he was able to immerse himself in Korean and Asian-American literature for the first time. Currently, he lives in New York City, teaching and writing.

바이링궐 에디션 한국 대표 소설 062
사랑하라, 희망 없이

2014년 6월 6일 초판 1쇄 인쇄 | 2014년 6월 13일 초판 1쇄 발행

지은이 윤영수 | 옮긴이 전승희 | **펴낸이** 김재범
감수 데이비드 윌리엄 홍 | **기획** 정은경, 전성태, 이경재
편집 정수인, 이은혜 | **관리** 박신영 | **디자인** 이춘희
펴낸곳 (주)아시아 | 출판등록 2006년 1월 27일 제406-2006-000004호
주소 서울특별시 동작구 서달로 161-1(흑석동 100-16)
전화 02.821.5055 | 팩스 02.821.5057 | **홈페이지** www.bookasia.org
ISBN 979-11-5662-018-1 (set) | 979-11-5662-026-6 (04810)
값은 뒤표지에 있습니다.

Bi-lingual Edition Modern Korean Literature 062
Love, Hopelessly

Written by Yun Young-su | **Translated by** Jeon Seung-hee
Published by Asia Publishers | 161-1, Seodal-ro, Dongjak-gu, Seoul, Korea
Homepage Address www.bookasia.org | **Tel.** (822).821.5055 | **Fax.** (822).821.5057
First published in Korea by Asia Publishers 2014
ISBN 979-11-5662-018-1 (set) | 979-11-5662-026-6 (04810)

바이링궐 에디션 한국 대표 소설 set 4